UNPLANNED

UNPLANNED

Historical Fiction Based on True-Life Experiences From World War II

John R. Cammidge

Columbus, Ohio

This book is a work of fiction. The names, characters and events in this book are the products of the author's imagination or are used fictitiously. Any similarity to real persons living or dead is coincidental and not intended by the author.

Unplanned

Published by Gatekeeper Press
2167 Stringtown Rd, Suite 109
Columbus, OH 43123-2989
www.GatekeeperPress.com

Copyright © 2020 by John R. Cammidge

Originally published in a different form during 2014 as *An Unplanned Encounter: Two Lives Forever Changed,* a work of fiction, using the author pen name of Jonathan R. Husband.

All rights reserved. Neither this book, nor any parts within it may be sold or reproduced in any form or by any electronic or mechanical means, including information storage and retrieval systems without permission in writing from the author. The only exception is by a reviewer, who may quote short excerpts in a review.

ISBN (paperback): 9781662903281
eISBN: 9781662903298

Library of Congress Control Number: 2020943505

PREFACE

This is a family story that needs to be written. It is dedicated to my mother who, at the age of 84, late one evening in London, explained to me for the first time the cause of my birth and the circumstances of my upbringing. I was born a fortnight before D-Day to a mother who lived with her parents in a home close to a military airfield in Yorkshire from where aircraft were flying bombing missions against Germany in preparation for the land invasion of Europe. Previous efforts to discover the truth of my existence from my mother had failed to illicit anything except assurances that the man she married in 1945 was my biological father. Even so, I had received evidence earlier in life that indicated that this statement was not true.

This is a World War II chronicle, set in Britain, which unravels the mystery of my childhood. It demonstrates the value of researching your family history before it is too late.

When my mother shared her account, she admitted to still being ashamed of what took place in the north of England at a time when she was single and aged 20. She pleaded with me not to investigate the story of my father and not to share the information with anyone, including my spouse, while she was still alive. I honoured her requests.

A year after this shattering confession, my mother passed away, permitting me to begin the research into the background of my father. The only information I had been given was his name, the name of the town and the name of the street in which he lived, the fact that he was married with two children and his wife was an opera singer, and my mother's claim that she had not seen him subsequent to my birth. These statements proved to be accurate, but I must caution readers that I trusted whatever my mother told me in the absence of anyone else still alive who could offer a contrary point of view.

With the help of Ancestry.com and a British genealogist, I eventually tracked down the address of my biological father's daughter. I met with her for the first time at the age of 66, and I uncovered the details of a new offshoot to my ancestral tree, but it was too late to contact my father who had died many years earlier, during August 1974.

For my mother's part, she left behind a detailed diary of her first 50 years of life, but it excluded any reference to those parts of her existence that caused her shame. None of what she told me that evening was included in her notebook. The story of my father is largely based on what my half-sister has shared with me, together with my personal surmises.

I have written the narrative involving my mother in the first person, since it was her story to tell and she shared with me her innermost thoughts. The remainder of the script is written in the third person because it rests on third-party information, and the fragments have been connected using imaginative writing that ultimately fictionalises the story; in addition, the names of the protagonists are made up.

You may feel that a novel like this must be sad and depressing. It is not. I received the greatest gift of all—the right to life—and I was raised by a very brave and courageous woman. Today, I am fortunate enough to enjoy close relationships with both sides of my family.

CHAPTER 1

It was a weekday early morning during mid-August 1943, and I was driving towards a small village in the East Riding of Yorkshire, England where I intended to move in with my parents. My name is Frances Mary and my journey began about 40 miles (65km) away in the city of Leeds, where I had lived for about two years performing my "war work", although I travelled home at least once a month to see my family. The war had given me a rare opportunity to make a career for myself because, prior to its occurrence, women generally were made to work at home. Therefore, for the first time in my life I enjoyed having a disposable income with which to dress myself and buy gifts for my family.

My trip was challenging because of petrol rationing, and there was always the risk of being attacked by enemy aeroplanes returning from their night-time attacks on Britain. I often drove in darkness along twisting country lanes, using only my car's side-lights to avoid my vehicle becoming a target. Visits from the Luftwaffe to Leeds were less frequent now, but no-one could predict the future. Thankfully, the United States had joined the battle and we seemed to be making progress. A few months earlier, 40 Luftwaffe aircraft had dropped incendiary devices and high explosive bombs on Leeds, killing 65 people and destroying about 100 houses.

After I relocated to Leeds, my parents had moved into the house towards which I was travelling, because the farm where they had lived previously was seized by the British government for the construction of a fighter airfield. Initially, we billeted workers in the farmhouse, which was untouched by the acquisition, but eventually my parents were forced to move elsewhere because of lack of income. Paradoxically, the new farm also had to relinquish most of its land for the building of an adjacent bomber airfield, and what acreage was left was taken over by the farm next door.

My father had always been a farmer, had grown up on a farm, had watched his siblings take up farming and had returned to this occupation after he was discharged from the army in March 1919, following the end of World War I. Because of his agricultural background, he was called up during May 1915 to be a horse driver for a transport platoon that carried ammunition and food supplies to the Front. Despite the daily dangers of serving in France, he survived, and his wartime duties came to an end when he was injured in battle and evacuated by ship back to Britain where he recuperated in hospital before being sent home.

To find a fresh source of income, my mother decided to accept lodgers into the new home, and the very important civil engineer in charge of planning for the construction of the nearby airfield had moved in to live with us. The house was also home to my two sisters; one is 18 months older than me and the other 4 years younger. I was 20 years of age and single.

Two years earlier, I was asked by the Navy, Army and Air Force Institutes (NAAFI—a company that manages the services provided for British Armed Forces) to live in Leeds and manage a canteen at a munitions training centre that daily served meals to over 3,000 workers. The canteen was open 24 hours each workday and served three shifts. Meals were planned in accordance with food-rationing restrictions, and I was responsible for hiring the staff and establishing their working hours. At the age of 18, this was a huge opportunity for me.

Starting in November 1940, establishments employing over 250 people were legally required to provide workers with hot meals. I organised a canteen serving in excess of this number during the construction of the airfield near our farm, and I did so well in the training centre that the NAAFI added two more facilities to my duties.

In Leeds I had lodged with my mother's cousin and worked virtually every day. Sundays off usually involved looking after my landlady's husband, who had suffered a stroke and was confined to a wheelchair; this required me to take him to church and then on to a local pub for a glass of beer before lunch. Eventually, physical exhaustion got the better of me, so I was told to leave my position in Leeds and transfer to the airfield canteen close to my parents' home and become its manager.

I was excited at the thought of living in the East Riding. My new job was smaller than the one in Leeds, so I expected that I would have much more time for social activities and I could resurrect my love of dancing. My boyfriend had been posted with his tank regiment to North Africa, so my plan was to go to dances with my sister and friends in order to stay loyal to him. It was a strange time, and by Christmas 1939 many fathers and sons, girls and boyfriends had been called up to fight. Women who chose not to join the armed forces volunteered to work in munitions factories, join the NAAFI or sign up for the country's Land Army.

I matured into womanhood during my time in Leeds. I think I became an attractive teenager, grew to a few inches over five feet, permed my brunette hair in the latest fashion, and I inherited sapphire-blue eyes and a graceful, straight nose from my mother. I was strong-willed and independent, and I possessed a high level of self-confidence because of my work. That evening, I was looking forward to replacing my NAAFI uniform with my slim-waisted, polka-dot tea-dress and going out dancing with my elder sister, her boyfriend and his cousin.

I had a passion for dreaming big and was always keen to advance my career, so even before I finished school I accepted my first job. Each evening I walked to the local fishermen's cottage on the bank of the nearby river and washed the men's supper dishes for sixpence a week. Sometimes the men took me to the river and allowed me to throw the fishing net to watch the weights sink, leaving the corks bobbing on the surface. Occasionally, we hauled in several salmon, but some nights nothing was caught, so I concluded that fishing was not a career for which I was suited.

Once I left school, I focused on acquiring the skills required to become a poultry farmer, and then I moved to the city of York where I was employed as a house-girl by a wealthy and prestigious family. There was never time to take a holiday during my childhood and adolescence, but I learned self-respect and the value of education from the people for whom I worked in the city. It was also here that I discovered my love of dancing. One of the maids and I would sneak out some evenings to attend dances in the city, and we particularly enjoyed the fox hunting club balls. It was after one of these events that our employer almost discovered our secret; we left the dancehall to discover that 3 inches (8cm) of snow had fallen, and we realised that we would leave tracks outside the house as evidence of our temporary escape. Fortunately, my colleague persuaded the gardener to clear away the evidence before the family arose from their beds the following morning.

Eventually, I had to return to live with my family when war broke out. On 3rd September 1939, I was attending church when, at 11am, the church warden arrived with a message for the parson; he inspected it and then read it to his congregation. It announced that a state of war had been declared between Britain and Germany because Hitler would not withdraw his troops from Poland. Some churchgoers cried, a few fainted and most knelt and prayed.

Evidence that we were at war quickly appeared. A few weeks after my return home, before Christmas 1939, bombs were dropped at nighttime on the village opposite ours on the other side of the river. Fires started, and their reflections in the water made the river turn red.

* * *

When my father lost his land, we kept as part of our original farm our large brick house on top of the hill, only 300 yards (275 metres) from the river, but we discovered that it could no longer provide us with an adequate income. We sold eggs, dressed chickens and the occasional duck, goose or turkey, and we also traded fruit and vegetables in the York market, but the combined proceeds were insufficient to support a family of five.

We found an alternative source of income, however. After initially losing the land, we were required to billet several workers in the farm house, and my father realised that there was money to be made in selling food directly to the people building the airfield. His idea was simple: move a hen house close to the construction site and convert it into a snack bar to serve the 200 labourers whose numbers were quickly growing. More workmen and tractor drivers arrived weekly, and army soldiers were eventually posted to guard the airfield. Once the hen house was relocated, my father and I organised the rest of family to make and sell homemade tea, coffee, soup, sandwiches and lemonade. We were so successful that I was able to employ several local villagers.

For workmen with duties on the opposite side of the airfield, food was taken to them every day by pony. Each morning, either my elder sister or I would ride the pony to the other side of the airfield and offer the men "drinkings" as they were called—the traditional Yorkshire word used for snacks taken to the fields for farm workers.

As the workforce grew, the construction firm provided us with a large Nissan hut (a shelter made of corrugated iron with a concrete floor) that we used to prepare the food as well as to sell it. Frankly, we were very successful, and I was proud of my entrepreneurial skills. Ultimately, when the air squadron arrived to take charge of the airfield, my business was taken over by the NAAFI, but to acknowledge my success, I was asked to accept the Leeds opportunity.

* * *

Eventually, I reached the end of my journey, and there was enough time to drop off my belongings at my parents' house before continuing to the airfield. My mother was in the midst of preparing breakfast and pleased to see me, while my elder sister was finishing her meal and rigged out in her British Land Girl uniform. She had joined the Women's Land Army after my parents moved to the East Riding, and she was one of nearly 80,000 women working on British farms in lieu of the men and boys who had gone off to fight. It was hard and dirty work involving long hours.

"Where's dad, and is our sister still in bed?" I casually asked.

"He's in the garden picking lettuces and radishes and trying to stop the birds from stealing his fruit. He's determined to prevent the blackbirds and robins from flying off with his raspberries this year," my mother replied.

"What about my younger sister?" I persisted, since I had not seen her for some time.

"She's already at the airfield, working in the canteen. I baked some bread this morning for her to take, and she should be working in the kitchen when you arrive."

Nodding, I told my mother that I had an 11am meeting with my deputy, but first I would go upstairs and wash.

"Am I still in the usual bedroom?" I queried, wondering if the lodger was still upstairs.

"Yes, but the lodger has left already," I was told.

I used a bedroom in the former servants' quarters, above the kitchen, which was accessed by a separate set of back stairs. The bedroom across the corridor belonged to the lodger, and opposite were the toilet and bathroom we shared. In the good old days, this was where the farm hands had lived, but now it provided accommodation for the two of us.

My mother respected the lodger and was proud of his reputation in the village as a very important person because of his work. I did not know him, although I had seen him on several occasions. I estimated him to be in his late twenties, had no understanding of farming, had an accent that must have come from close to Birmingham and was very proud of his family.

On the way to my bedroom, I noticed that his door was open and peeped inside his room. Nothing was out of place; the bed was carefully made, his shoes were lined up tidily alongside the bed, his clothes were put away in cupboards, and even his few personal belongings were neatly organised on the dressing table.

Before departing, I selected my slim-fitting, polka-dot tea-dress for the dance and hung it up outside the wardrobe to smooth out the wrinkles. Once refreshed, I waved goodbye to my father, who was still in the garden, and drove off towards the airfield, about a mile away. The deputy who worked for me at the canteen, Joan Sykes, had arranged an 11am meeting to discuss staffing levels for the coming weeks. Recruitment was difficult because many women believed the airfield to be a target for German bombers, and they were afraid of finding themselves stranded when the air-raid sirens sounded.

CHAPTER 2

The Number 4 Bomber Command Air Commodore was driving that same mid-August morning to meet with the civil engineer responsible for constructing the airfield next to where Frances Mary's parents lived. The facility was urgently needed to add to the country's bombing capacity prior to the invasion of mainland Europe, although the Commodore had heard that its completion was going to take longer than expected.

He wondered if the delay was intentional because of his refusal to grant home leave to the civil engineer in charge of the complex. The engineer had asked to visit his family on the other side of England following the birth of his daughter, but any delay in completing the work was unacceptable because Number 77 squadron was waiting to move to the new airfield and release its own base to two French squadrons.

It would be fair to say that most people disliked the Air Commodore. He was a formidable person, from a prestigious and well-educated family, who imposed exacting standards on his subordinates and was unwilling to compromise. People were allowed no flexibility, but they nonetheless respected him, even when they did not agree with him, and he considered anyone below the rank of a commissioned officer to be of inferior intellect.

He oversaw the operations of approximately ten airfields that were used by a dozen squadrons flying heavy bombers, primarily the Handley Page 'Halifax'. This was a four-engine heavy bomber that formed a major component of Bomber Command. This morning, however, he was at the wheel of his black Vauxhall travelling eastwards into the glare of the early morning sun to investigate the only airfield under his jurisdiction that was yet to become operational.

The Commodore's six-foot frame fit comfortably into the driver's seat, thanks to his slim build, and his authority was signified by the uniform he wore, including the blue-grey peaked cap with its black mohair band and gilded ornamentation. His upper lip displayed the customary airman's moustache.

The sun strained at the morning's horizon to produce a whitish humid sky, and thunderstorms were forecast for the afternoon. The lanes and fields of the countryside were quiet, and it seemed that the birds were anticipating a change in the weather. Swallows were flying low to catch their breakfast of insects, starlings remained perched in their shelters, rather than dispersing to feed, and even the rookeries were quieter than normal. The Air Commodore hoped he would be back in his York headquarters before the bad weather arrived.

There had been an argument a few days earlier. The civil engineer had asked to go home, a day's journey away, to spend time with his wife and newborn daughter. Headquarters had refused to approve the leave, stressing that it was more important for him to stay at the airfield to complete his responsibilities. Bombing the enemy was currently Britain's main form of attack against the Germans, and the more landing strips that could be opened up, the better. During July 1943, the Royal Air Force had finished its five-month Battle of the Ruhr that disrupted German steel production, water supplies and arms manufacture, and shortly thereafter had participated with the Americans in Operation Gomorrah, a bombing campaign over Hamburg that killed approximately 21,000 women, 13,000 men and 8,000 children. There were eight days and seven nights of intensive bombing, involving several hundred aircraft, and the resulting firestorms created winds that swept up people like dried leaves. It was the heaviest assault in the history of aerial warfare before Hiroshima.

* * *

Unplanned

The outline of the Yorkshire Wolds stretched ahead of the Air Commodore as his car made deliberate progress towards his destination. To his left and right was the flat Vale of York, a rich agricultural area bounded by the Howardian Hills, with the Wolds to the east, the Pennines to the west, the Vale of Mowbray to the north, and the remnants of a former ice age, the Escrick moraine, to the south.

Ever since the Royal Air Force Expansion Plan of 1935, there had been non-stop building of new airfields in Britain, and especially in Yorkshire. By the time World War II began, 100 new airfields had been built or were in the process of being completed. A requirement was that each new air base should be as close to Berlin as possible, and consequently sites were chosen that were on or near the same latitude as Berlin. If a location was deemed suitable, the land was requisitioned under the 1939 Emergency Powers Act, and by 1943 Yorkshire and Lincolnshire had become known as the aircraft carriers of Britain.

Number 4 Bomber Command was responsible for airfields located in the east and south of Yorkshire. The group had been reorganised in March 1943 and given ten bomber airfields and a dozen bomber squadrons to supervise. The Air Commodore's duty was to make sure that all airfields were operational in accordance with the Royal Air Force's timetable.

Today, the Air Commodore was visiting the only airfield under Number 4 Bomber Command that was still not functioning. As a substation, it was supposed to be one of three bases grouped under a parent airfield, and it had been scheduled to open by year-end 1943. However, the civil engineer in charge of planning had told the authorities that there were construction difficulties so his airfield could not open before early 1944.

The Air Commodore's vehicle continued its journey with the persistent throb of a tiny engine announcing its passing. The headlights were not lit, so the horizontal strips of the masks covering them were not in use, the side indicators no longer emitted the color of orange peel, and the tail lamps had been dimmed to comply with blackout rules. Fear of an invasion had led to the implementation of the blackout during September 1939, and while anxieties had lessened in recent months as Germany focused on its Russian front, Air-Raid Patrol wardens and eagle-eyed neighbours were quick to report transgressions.

A bottle of whisky lay on the back seat of the car, a gift for the person to whom he had refused to grant family leave, and he hoped that it would motivate the civil engineer to accept the decision and expedite the construction. There was already speculation that the Allied invasion of northern Europe was under preparation, and while no one said much, everyone realised that the advance contributions from Bomber Command were essential for success.

Airfield construction had continued throughout the war. It was not unusual to see men working on these sites, and contractors relied on local people for knowledge to understand the geography, terrain, soil and drainage. Farmers, who only weeks earlier had received government letters requisitioning their land, were now driving tractors and leading horses to tear down hedges and remove debris. Farm buildings were bulldozed, and the rubble was used to level the uneven land. Large trees were cut down using crosscut saws, and roots and trunks were splintered with explosives. Once the land was cleared, heavy equipment moved in to construct the buildings and lay the foundations for the three paved runways required on each bomber airfield.

The Air Commodore advanced along the narrow country lanes, with hedges reaching towards each other across single-track roads. The car passed occasional farms silhouetted sharply by the sunrise. Soon he passed over the tracks of the York to Beverley railway line and passed close to a station that had been closed many decades earlier.

Signs of early-morning activity included cattle noisily making their way to milking sheds, and the clucking of hens as they gave up their overnight deposit of eggs. Farm windows were darkened by blackout curtains, early morning mist bedewed the damp grass, and the air's stillness magnified the sound of sheep bleating across the fields.

The driver had no idea of the history of the places through which he was driving; he knew only the route to be taken. Most road signs had been removed because of the invasion scare during the summer of 1940, and those that remained were often pointing in the wrong direction. The occasional dark outline of a church would mark the site of an approaching village, typically clustered around common land, and these hamlets bore evidence of past invaders from continental Europe, including Romans, Anglo-Saxons, Vikings, Danes and Normans who had left behind their language in the names of the villages.

Soon the Air Commodore found himself driving north-east towards his destination. The sun was higher in the sky by now, but the change in direction meant he avoided facing the summertime glare. The car crested a hill composed of boulder clay, and as the climb flattened out, the driver found himself perched high and overlooking a flat landscape.

In the distance, the outline of a village could be seen, its lone church standing upright and silent. The ringing of church bells had been banned in mid-1940, with the directive that the bells should be rung only as a signal that enemy troops were invading the country. An exception to this rule had been made a few months earlier, however, when during November 1942 Britain had celebrated the victory of its Eighth Army at El Alamein. Winston Churchill believed this battle was the turning point in the war and ordered church bells to ring across Britain. As he later said, "Before Alamein, we never had a victory; after Alamein, we never had a defeat."

Ahead of the car, to the left and at the base of the moraine, lay the driver's destination. What had once been common land for the local villages was now an emerging airfield. The layout of the three concrete runways could be discerned, and the perimeter track around the airfield was visible. Some of the dispersal pans to be used by scattering the aircraft during an enemy attack could be seen, and other buildings were taking shape. The driver sighed in relief that he had arrived without difficulty.

His intention was to sit down with the civil engineer, George Luckett, and find out exactly what was going on. He had given Mr Luckett approval to invite to the meeting his technical adviser, an American of Belgian descent named Michael Fromm. Apparently, this person could explain the true causes of the delay.

The car and driver descended the hill, turned left onto a narrow approach road, and stopped at the gate to the new airfield.

"Are you expecting me?" asked the Air Commodore.

"Certainly, sir," was the guard's sharp reply, as he gave his salute. "Please park in the paved area of the car park, and Mr Luckett will meet you outside the contractors' canteen."

The Air Commodore parked his vehicle, picked up the bottle of whisky and made his way to the Control Tower, which was close to the canteen.

Chapter 3

Thirty-year old George Luckett was an experienced civil engineer, considered smart and intelligent by his colleagues so that his subordinates rarely disagreed with his recommendations. He looked like an "expert" with his circular-framed spectacles, the briar pipe languishing in his mouth and the sports jacket and flannels that he usually wore. His appointment as planning director for this particular airfield occurred during 1942, and his responsibilities included assisting with reconstruction design at other airfields, controlled by Number 4 Bomber Command, that either required expanded facilities or where the infrastructure had been damaged by attacks from enemy aircraft.

He was a little under six feet tall, possessed an angular, almost gaunt face, and engaged people with his smile and twinkling eyes. There were early signs of balding on both temples, and his brownish hair was swept back in a short-back-and-sides style, parted on the left side. He missed his family and remained angry that the Air Commodore had refused him permission to visit his newborn daughter. Earlier in the year, while she was pregnant, his wife had travelled to see him at his lodgings but now, with the addition of a second child, she could no longer visit and he had not been able to return home for about a year.

He believed he was being punished for something that was beyond his control, since the delay in construction was due to drainage problems and, in particular, the site for the three landing strips that had flooded during recent storms, not because of any unforeseen planning delays. His technical adviser would show that these were the reasons and that it was unfair to blame him for the inadequate land assessments and the wet summer weather.

* * *

George came from a family whose homes were in the West Midlands. His father had been a pawnbroker in the town next to where George currently lived, and after George was born, he had become a school inspector as well as serving in the local special police constabulary. He gained a formidable reputation for tracking down school truants and incarcerating them in Approved Schools (residential places for convicted youths or those who were beyond the control of their parents), where discipline was tough and physical work onerous. George's mother was an only child and her family was well off. They built and owned houses, and as a child, George remembered accompanying his mother when she collected the rents.

The local boys' grammar school had educated George and taught him how to play the violin and piano, but both instruments were now left at home. He had enjoyed his frequent childhood holidays to Scotland, Wales and the south of England, and he especially loved the Dorset coast and day trips by ferry to Jersey and Guernsey. However, now that he was married, and in the midst of a war, touring the country was no longer practical.

He elected not to go to university but to stay at home to train as a civil engineer. He worked during the day and studied at night on a Day Release scheme for one day a week to attend the local technical college. He was sponsored by a work colleague as a student member of the British Institute of Civil Engineers, and he had been employed by several town planning offices before the war.

For leisure, he joined the local operatic society where he met his future wife, the daughter of a lock maker. She was the lead singer in the Gilbert and Sullivan opera company, and he used his artistic talents to become the stage manager and court her. They married during 1938 and lived in a home close to both sets of parents until he transferred to east Yorkshire to construct the airfield. As a qualified civil engineer, he was excused conscription in the British armed forces.

East Yorkshire was a strange place to him. It was full of farms and small hamlets, and very different from the bustling cities, decrepit housing slums and dirty factories with which he was familiar. It seemed like a more dangerous place because the Luftwaffe was more active in this part of Britain, and had even attacked nearby York just after his arrival. The attack involved 70 German aircraft that had dive-bombed ordinary civilians on the streets and strafed them with machine gun fire, then bombed strategic targets, supposedly in retaliation for the Royal Air Force's attack on the historic towns of Lubeck and Rostock in Germany.

He missed his family but settled down to fulfil his mission. His first child was born only weeks before he came to Yorkshire, and his daughter was born during June 1943. He had found very comfortable lodgings adjacent to the airfield, although there was little to do in the evenings when he was not at work. His landlady treated him as a very important person, spoke of him to others as being the "bee's knees" (highly admired), and provided him with whatever he requested.

The airfield was an exhilarating ten-minute cycle ride down the hill most mornings, except when it was frosty, foggy or wet. The evening return was not something he looked forward to, as it was slow and physically exhausting to cycle uphill.

On this particular day, he had arranged to meet with the Air Commodore in charge of this particular airfield, and he anticipated a very difficult conversation. His structural engineer would be available to explain the geophysical problems that were the cause of the delay during construction. For example, the weight of the new bomber aircraft required concrete landing strips to be sturdier than those originally planned, and there were site drainage problems that the land surveyors had never identified.

* * *

His assistant, Michael Fromm, was twenty-three years old, and two years earlier had arrived from California to help the British win the war. His father was a Belgian refugee who had emigrated to the United States after World War I, and who had recently lost contact with his relatives because of the German invasion of Belgium. Michael was motivated by his father's World War I experience and believed he could assist his family in Belgium recover their freedom by supporting the British war effort. He spoke nearly perfect German because his father came from the German-speaking area of Belgium, and his mother was originally from Germany. She and her family had moved to the United States early in 1914 to avoid religious persecution; they had originally settled in Ohio, but they moved to California when local anti-German sentiment surfaced during the World War I years.

Michael's father had fought with the Belgian army alongside the British after Antwerp fell to the Germans in October 1914, as Belgian neutrality had been threatened when Germany insisted on the safe passage of its soldiers through Belgium in order to invade France from the north. The Belgian authorities had refused the request, arguing that a German presence would be a violation of international law, and threatened retaliation to any incursion of the Germans by using all means available to them. As the fighting broke out, the Belgians fought more stubbornly and courageously than anticipated, and they were able to delay the German advance into northern France. The country's resistance also gave Britain the excuse it needed to declare war on Germany during August 1914.

It was a bitter war, with some of the harshest treatment reserved for the Belgians. As Germany occupied their country, rumours grew of atrocities committed against the local population, including the burning of houses, the killing of old men, deportation of adults to Germany to work in the factories, and even allegations that small boys were having their thumbs sliced off so that they would be of no future military use. Eventually Fromm Senior fled to Holland to avoid internment by the Germans. He was one of several thousand military personnel who disguised themselves as civilians and were housed in a variety of renovated barracks, brickyards, tent villages, churches and private houses on arrival. Hygiene was poor and overcrowding standard, but he found work as a farmhand.

Daytime consisted of hard labour, nighttime was a state of boredom, and the local Dutch community remained suspicious of the intentions of their uninvited guests. Eventually he concluded that he must move to England, where he hoped he could make a more direct contribution to the war effort. He arrived in early spring 1916, on the deck of a fishing trawler that docked at the port of North Shields, close to the city of Newcastle in the north of England, and he quickly found work at a nearby munitions factory.

Despite the warm welcome on the dockside, he soon discovered that the Belgian and English communities were suspicious of each other and were kept apart; he also learned that work in the factories was noisy, hazardous and subject to close supervision and discipline. He was given accommodation in a self-contained village that housed only Belgians, conformed with Belgian law and was guarded by Belgian policemen. He considered his work to be of value, but both working and living conditions were intolerable so he searched for new opportunities.

The United States was on the brink of joining the war (which it did on 6th April 1917) and needed to strengthen its armed forces. Its merchant ships and passenger vessels were being attacked by Germany, and the country was largely unprepared to participate. Consequently, its armed forces were accepting volunteers to serve, as well as relying on the draft and conscription. By volunteering as a trained soldier, and one who could speak English, Flemish and German, he hoped to qualify after the war for fast-track US residency. As the war ended, he and his family were given approval to emigrate to the United States, and at first they decided to settle in Wisconsin which already had a substantial Belgian population, many of whom were descendants of farmers and farm laborers who had moved to the United States in the mid-nineteenth century due to land shortages and the potato blight in Belgium.

However, after a short period of farm labouring, Fromm Senior decided to seek his fortune in California and moved to Sacramento. He was fortunate enough to find employment at a newly opened local Air Force base, and after the required number of weeks of training, he became a qualified aircraft mechanic. He fell in love with a girl he met and they married.

* * *

Some of Michael's American friends chose to join the Royal Air Force, but he decided to work for the British Air Ministry Directorate of General Works that managed the affairs of the Royal Air Force. He was a graduate in materials engineering from a local California state college, and he had gained prior experience by helping reactivate two Sacramento airfields.

The Directorate produced design specifications for British aircraft and air bases, chose new airfield sites and employed civil contractors to complete their construction. Beginning a few years earlier, it was given responsibility for the largest civil engineering programme ever undertaken in Britain; it was estimated that this Ministry controlled a labour force of around 60,000 men and that, by 1943, construction involved some 800 contracts distributed among 136 firms.

When Michael first arrived, he worried that his enlistment would jeopardise his United States citizenship because, before America officially entered World War II in December 1941, it was illegal for a United States citizen to join the armed forces of a foreign nation. These fears had more or less gone away by mid-1942 as, by then, the United States was participating in the war and had begun constructing its own airfields across south-east England. While observing Air Ministry standards, the United States Army used its own Engineering Battalions to construct some of these airfields.

Michael was very self-assured, trim and gracious towards other people and well-dressed most of the time. He loved company but equally enjoyed being on his own. He was loyal to his bosses, although direct and decisive. If there was anything you could remember about him, it was his large, deep-set, coffee-brown eyes. He had broken up with his girlfriend before leaving the United States, and now enjoyed the social opportunities offered by the East Riding of Yorkshire. He loved the open air, enjoyed music and motorbikes, and he would go to the pictures and to local dances if he could find a girl to accompany him. If he could not, he and George would spend much of their time in local pubs. Presently, Michael was dating a teenage farm girl whose parents were not particularly happy with the romance.

At the airfield, he was affectionately known as "the Yank", although in Europe he preferred to think of himself as Belgian. After working on several military projects around London, he transferred to this airfield and was billeted a few miles away at a posting inn (post house) dating back to Tudor times. It was a fifteen-minute motor-cycle ride to the airfield.

Initially, he had used a taxi for transport, but he had been unnerved when he read about a similar taxi operating in the neighbourhood that had its headlights in use early one morning when it was strafed by a Luftwaffe bomber returning to Germany. In response, he bought himself a 1940 BSA M23 Silver Star at the local British Small Arms' motorbike dealership and had used it ever since to get around. He possessed insufficient funds to purchase the bike outright, so he had to buy it via a hire-purchase agreement, or what the British called "the never-never".

On this particular morning, his bike seemed eager to take him to the airfield where he knew George would be waiting for him. He had been warned about the sensitivity of the meeting, and he knew that it was important for him to exonerate George by describing the geophysical limitations of the site that had caused the delay in construction. He knew his boss did not like the Air Commodore, who had a reputation for being pompous and inflexible, and that he would do his best to support his friend and boss.

As his motorbike reached the brow of the hill, he looked across the fields at the partly-completed Control Tower, and in the distance he could just make out the profile of George and another man whom he assumed was the Air Commodore.

CHAPTER 4

By the time Michael Fromm had padlocked his motorbike and reached the Control Tower, the two men had disappeared into the nearby canteen. The kitchen served cooked meals, snacks and refreshments, and the staff was still serving breakfast when Michael walked into the dining area. Electric cables were strung overhead to deliver power, water was brought in from a nearby public water supply and adequate sanitation had been installed. He stopped to accept a bowl of porridge, served by a pretty teenage girl, and his appetite was aroused by the sound and smell of sizzling bacon.

The menu benefitted from the goodwill of the local villagers who supplied fresh eggs, some of the bacon, milk, butter, bread and even tomatoes at this time of the year. There were also locally baked pastries and cakes. Rationing had begun in January 1940, and at first it had affected butter, bacon, sugar and tea; a little later it included meat, milk, cheese, eggs, lard, jams and rice. Bread remained exempt, as did fish, potatoes and most fruits and vegetables, and the daily menu in the canteen depended on what was available from the farms.

Michael quickly ordered eggs, bacon, toast and a mug of tea. His boss, George and the stranger were seated at the far end of the room, and he walked over to join them once his food was served.

"Take a seat," invited George, "and meet the Air Commodore from headquarters." His guest appeared sullen and not very talkative, but ignoring these characteristics, George turned to the Air Commodore and introduced Michael.

"This is Mr Fromm, our 'Yank' from California. He's going to explain our technical difficulties that are delaying the opening."

The Air Commodore nodded to Michael, and he seemed to have the attention of almost everyone in the canteen because of his uniform. One of the waitresses brought over a pot of tea, a jug of milk and a bowl of sugar, and placed them in front of the men, but all three of them showed a reluctance to start the conversation. It felt as if an unpleasant dialogue lay ahead.

Ultimately, it was the Air Commodore who broke the silence, laid out a map of the airfield on the table, and began his probe. "So, where's the problem and why wasn't I told earlier? It's totally unacceptable that you allowed the project to overrun its completion date."

George began defensively. "If the land survey had been more accurate before we began construction, the problems would never have arisen. We would have configured the air strips differently, but that's too late now."

"Why?" demanded the Air Commodore.

"Because we'd have to knock down most of what we've already built to accommodate the new layout, and that would take longer than what we are recommending," was George's answer.

"So, what exactly has gone wrong?" The Air Commodore had a natural mistrust of civilians and continued to be suspicious of what he was being told,

George asked Michael to explain, which he did.

"You've probably seen that fabrication of the buildings is underway and that several structures have been completed," said Michael. "Also, the perimeter fence to keep out cattle is finished, we are underway with the construction of the dispersal pans to protect aircraft during an attack, bomb storage areas and air raid shelters are in place, and the excavation for the landing strips is underway. The problem is the clay; there's too much of it and it's causing a drainage problem. There's flooding on the landing strips and in some of the dispersal pans. We have to overcome the drainage problems to protect flight operations, and that will take time. Also, the air strips will take longer to complete because the thickness of the concrete has to be increased to accommodate the much heavier weight of the new aircraft."

"So, what's the revised timeline if you do all of this?" snarled a disappointed Air Commodore.

"The original plan was January, but now it seems more likely that it will be April before we can start moving in 'planes and pilots," George replied.

Clearly the Air Commodore was dissatisfied, and although there was little he could do about the situation, he continued his criticism. "Well, you should know that everyone in headquarters is very displeased with your performance. You've created a serious situation, and everyone will have to stay on-site until the construction is completed. No-one is allowed home leave until the job is done."

"But that's unfair." George felt vindicated but was very unhappy that his leave was still being denied. "We didn't create the problem, and I've not seen my family for six months. It will be more than a year before I can see them again."

"You're not going anywhere," replied the Air Commodore. "No-one leaves this place, including you. We can't afford the risk of you coming to some harm while travelling. Do you understand me?"

"But it's safer near my home than here," George argued. "There's been no bombing close to my family since last year."

"There are still risks," responded the Air Commodore, "and you are safer here than elsewhere. Who would want to attack a non-operational airfield, with nothing of importance in the nearby village? You're living in one of the safest places in Yorkshire, and if it will help, I've brought you a bottle of whisky to lessen your disappointment."

There was little else to say, as the Air Commodore handed the George the bottle of whisky. All in all, it had been an unpleasant meeting and no-one felt satisfied with the outcome. George told Michael to accompany the Air Commodore back to his car, and then abruptly left for his office, carrying the bottle of whisky.

* * *

I left my parents' home and was at the airfield in time for my appointment with Joan Sykes. Immediately, I went to the kitchen to greet my younger sister who was busy peeling potatoes, and I found Joan finalising the lunch menu. Her helpers were preparing sandwiches of sardines, beetroot, cucumber and corned beef, as well as the alternative of a hot meal; today it was meat stew with mashed potatoes and carrots. She welcomed me with a big smile.

I was fortunate to have Joan as my assistant. She was a portly, homely woman, about my height, with a round, florid face. She had lived in the village all her life, so she knew everyone, and she was highly respected. I trusted her to manage the daily operations of the kitchen, while I was responsible for procuring food and equipment, recruiting new workers and organising the work schedule.

"So, how was the journey?" she asked me. "Did you encounter any of those German 'planes?"

I told her it had been an easy drive, and it seemed that there was less bombing than in the past. The greatest worry I had was when driving close to a river, as these were often used as navigation aids by German pilots who sometimes machine-gunned whatever they saw on the road, or dropped any remaining bombs they carried on anything that looked like a target.

"So, have you heard today's news?" asked Joan.

I confessed I had not and was curious. "What is it?"

"Well, the top brass from RAF headquarters was here earlier today to find out why it's taking longer than planned to open the airfield. Betty, the new waitress, served his table and says she heard both the head of planning and his technical adviser being reprimanded. Apparently, the delay is caused by the muddy conditions. Anyone who has farmed here knows the land is always waterlogged and that the clay is heavy and impervious. Anyway, the announcement is that we won't be operational before April next year."

"What happened to them?" I asked, worried that my mother might have lost the income of her lodger.

"They're fine, except for damaged egos, and they've been told no-one can leave the airfield until it's operational. Mr Luckett is very annoyed, and we haven't seen him since the conversation. The challenge for us is to staff this place for an extra three months, and it won't be easy to find workers and keep them. Maybe we can hire from other villages and transport people here by bus?"

At that moment, Joan was interrupted by Betty who asked if there were any changes to plans to construct Nissan huts in the village. Her mum was annoyed that one was being erected at the village's lane end, and it would be an eyesore for everyone coming to and leaving the community. If the Royal Air Force was going to ignore the villagers' needs, she was not going to allow her daughter to work in the canteen. Joan could give no assurances.

"That's our biggest problem," Joan claimed. "Not only will some ladies not show up when the air-raid sirens sound, but some parents are stopping their girls from working here."

I nodded my understanding. There were ongoing staffing problems and I needed to discuss them with the NAAFI. It might be necessary to recruit help from outlying villages and use the support of local churches to find volunteers.

I thanked Joan for the update and said I would be at work the following morning. For now, I was tired, having left Leeds early in the morning, and wanted to grab some sleep before I went dancing with my sister. If Joan did not mind, I needed to go home for some rest. She agreed.

CHAPTER 5

I GAVE MY YOUNGER sister a lift home to save her from getting wet, as we were chased up the hill by a thunderstorm, with its flashes of lightning and crashes of thunder, and then it began to rain. As I pulled into the driveway, I saw my father run from the garden through a torrential downpour, shouting that he was going next door to help herd some cattle into a shelter. My mother had returned from an outbuilding, where she had been washing clothes, to the kitchen where she had started to prepare dinner for the lodger. Shortly afterwards, the rain ended, the weather turned cooler and less humid and the sun came out.

I made myself a cup of tea before clambering upstairs to my room to sleep. It felt good to lie on my own bed.

I do not know what time the lodger returned. Apparently, he had come upstairs, left his work papers in his bedroom and then cycled to the public telephone kiosk on the other side of the village green to call his wife. Next, he rode to the end of the village to inspect the Nissan huts that the residents were complaining about. They looked fine to him.

A surprise waited for him when he returned home. My mother was preparing his favourite meal of egg and chips, followed by Charlotte russe, a sweet comprising slices of sponge cake arranged in a circle, then the centre filled with custard and cream mixed with strawberries and rum. Once the meal was over, he retired upstairs to write letters and drink his whisky.

I must have been woken up around 6pm by my elder sister calling from the bottom of the stairs, telling me to start getting ready for the dance. Once the rain had stopped, she had cycled home from the farm with the news that her boyfriend would drive us to the dance and his cousin would be my partner for the evening.

"OK," I shouted back, "I'll get up now."

I still felt grimy because of the morning's drive, and hot and sticky because of the summer humidity, so I decided to take a bath. Bathing was a relatively new luxury for me, as until I moved to Leeds, taking a bath meant filling a zinc metal tub with hot water and cleaning myself using coal-tar soap (an orange antiseptic cleanser) once a week on Fridays in front of the fire. Consequently, this evening it was a pleasant change to pamper myself with warm water and proper soap, and I did not want to leave the bath, even though it was relatively shallow as I had to limit the amount of water I used.

We were expected to restrict our use of water, and this was just one more aspect of our lives that had changed because of the war. The Royal family encouraged British people to bathe only when necessary, and never to take a bath in water more than five inches deep.

The hot water relaxed my body and relieved the stress of the day. Unfortunately, I eventually had to leave its warmth and dry myself before sprinkling myself with talcum powder, wrapping myself in a large towel and returning to my bedroom to dress. On the way, I heard the lodger calling in my direction, and it was only then that I realised he was back in the house.

"Is that you Frances Mary? Come in and share some whisky with me; I'm celebrating an awful day at the airfield!"

"I can't," I called back. "I'm going dancing and have to get dressed; maybe some other time."

He was not discouraged by my answer. "There won't be another time. The whisky will be gone today. It will only take five minutes."

With that, his bedroom door opened and he waved me inside. I hesitated, feeling sorry for him because of the day's events, and I did not want to upset my mother by being rude towards him, so I entered, still wearing only my towel.

I think he was surprised by my lack of clothes. Even so, he looked sad and lonely, and I felt even sorrier for him. He had suffered a difficult day and was missing his family, whereas I was about to go out dancing.

He was in his shirt sleeves, and he sat me down on the side of the bed, gave me a glass of whisky and asked me to read a letter that he was sending to his bosses at the construction firm. It asked that he be allowed to visit his family and criticised the Air Commodore for refusing him permission. He showed me pictures of his wife and baby daughter, so I looked at them and politely told him I was sorry.

That is when it happened. He grabbed me and tried to kiss me. I resisted, but he was stronger and I did not know what to do. Then there was a sudden blur of activity as he pulled off the towel and pushed me backwards onto the bed. I consented to nothing, but that did not seem to matter. He fumbled with his own clothes and told me not to make a noise.

During the assault, although I resisted as much as I could, I stayed quiet because my parents were in the kitchen below and I did not want them to hear. I knew they would be upset to think that I had gone into his bedroom, especially as I was wearing only a towel, and I hoped it would be over soon. It was humiliating, and I thought it was my fault, so I was deeply afraid of what people would say if they ever found out.

Eventually it was over. He handed me back the towel, apologised for his actions and instructed me not to tell anyone about what had just taken place. I could not imagine that he would say anything to people he knew in case his wife found out. I left the room in a hurry, feeling very upset, and wondering what I was supposed to have done. I retraced my steps to the bathroom, washed myself and brushed my hair, and prepared to go downstairs.

It was inconceivable that I should tell anyone. I thought no-one would believe me, and if they did, they would say it was my fault. The incident was best kept a secret, and I hoped the memory of it would soon fade away. I returned to my bedroom, put on the polka-dot dance-dress and went to meet my sister, her boyfriend and his cousin.

From the beginning, I wished the evening would end quickly so that I could be back in bed at home. I found it easier to talk than to dance, so I was grateful when my escort introduced me to a girl similar in age to myself. She was accompanied by an American whom I had seen around the airfield, she lived on a farm next to my sister's boyfriend's farm between our village and the next one, and we briefly talked about her work as a member of the Women's Land Army.

Although I have always loved dancing, tonight it was stressful. I did not enjoy the feeling of being close to another man, even though he was polite and interesting. I kept telling myself that the assault had not happened, that it was all in my imagination. Then fears of my parents finding out took over. After all, I had gone into the lodger's room wearing only a towel, I had stupidly agreed to share some whisky with him, and I had not resisted strenuously enough or run away when he grabbed me. I was convinced that no-one would believe my story, and who knew what the lodger might say in his defence? He would probably deny everything. Therefore, I thought silence was my best strategy, and I should try to forget the incident and let my life continue as if nothing had happened.

It was a great relief when the dance was over, and I was taken home and found myself alone in my bedroom. Once more, I washed myself thoroughly, snuggled underneath the sheets and tried to forget about the events of the early evening. However, my night's sleep was disturbed, and I did not want to rise in the morning, but I had to be at the airfield to help serve breakfast. I left the house before the lodger, and I hoped I would not see him that day.

* * *

The days passed and no-one said anything that led me to believe that my secret had not been discovered. Mr Luckett continued to appear lonely, and his assistant's relationship with the farm girl became more serious. Thus, the lodger had no one to go out with and, since the authorities did not change their decision on his home leave, he seemed to immerse himself in his work.

The remaining summer weeks passed rapidly, with plenty of sunshine, albeit the weather remained humid and thundery. It was soon harvesting time, about the only thing that had not changed because of the war, except that there were mainly women in the fields rather than men. At the same time, my elder sister pleased my parents by announcing that she would marry her boyfriend at the beginning of the following year.

Joan continued to support me at work, and we found enough women to staff the canteen as the construction continued. I occasionally saw the lodger at work, but we both went out of our way to move in opposite directions and not say anything to each other. During the evenings, he was busy giving presentations in the village, explaining the zoning plans for the Nissan huts. The drainage work progressed well, with additional scrapers and diggers brought in to excavate ditches to drain off the water.

By now, there were more bombers leaving Yorkshire for Germany than coming in the opposite direction. Rumour had it that Germany was preparing to replace aircraft with pilotless 'planes called "flying bombs". These were known as "doodlebugs" and were to be launched from ramps aimed towards their target, and would carry significant amounts of high-grade, blast-effective explosive. Efforts to disrupt these plans had begun, and hundreds of aircraft were sent to a small island in the Baltic Sea to bomb what was believed to be the research centre for this new weapon.

There were also flights south across Germany to bomb armament and munitions factories in preparation for what was to become D-Day. A Messerschmitt factory and a large ball-bearing plant were bombed. In Italy there was carpet bombing of Foggia on 19th August 1943, British troops invaded mainland Italy on 3rd September 1943 and Italy unilaterally surrendered on 8th September 1943.

I had not spoken to anyone about my encounter with the lodger, and memories of the incident were fading. I still attended the occasional dance, but I avoided relationships with men. Letters came from my boyfriend, who was now part of the invasion of Italy, and it pleased me to know that he was still alive.

Harvesting on the farms got underway. Horse- or tractor-drawn reaper-binders were dusted off, oiled and moved into the fields in readiness to start work. It soon began, as the hot summer weather had turned the cereal crops golden and dry. Young and old, the villagers gathered to celebrate bringing in the harvest in the fields, as well as to gather the new sources of food becoming available in the hedgerows. Picking blackberries, hazel nuts and crab apples was enjoyed by the children, both boys and girls.

The farmers who were too old or exempt from military service operated the harvesting machinery, while the women, young and old, followed behind gathering sheaves of wheat or barley, and building stooks of six or eight sheaves. Arranging the direction of each stook from east to west was necessary to catch the prevailing drying winds. A few days later, once the drying process was complete, the farmers returned to the fields to gather the sheaves for storage in a barn until the annual visit of the threshing machine.

Harvesting also provided a new source of meat. As fields lost their crops, the reaper would disturb rabbits and hares, but their freedom was brief. The farmers' guns were accurate, the dogs retrieved the bodies, and meals of rabbit stew were prepared. We shot so many that there was more than enough for the villagers to eat. The excess was donated to the airfield, and rabbit casserole was added to the menu in the canteen. With bacon, carrots and onions, the meal was a huge improvement over the corned beef and fried SPAM (Special Processed American Meat) usually on offer.

At times, Michael Fromm would visit the fields to collect his girlfriend, since she helped with the harvest. Her parents remained troubled that she was dating an American, but they accepted the fact that they could not do anything about it. They could not understand most of what Michael said, and he had given up trying to understand their Yorkshire dialect. The noise of his motorbike could be heard from a distance when he collected his girlfriend to take her home.

It was a time for celebration. Some of the sheaves of corn were donated to the village church, along with baskets of fruit, vegetables and flowers, to celebrate Harvest Festival Sunday. As country people, it was important for us to honour the traditions of bringing in the harvest. This year, the church service took place during September and was followed by the feast of St Michael to mark the end of summer and the beginning of winter (which would end on Christmas Day).

Michaelmas Day (29th September) was the date when agricultural labourers traditionally presented themselves for hire for the coming year. It was also a special day for the airfield workers. It was a time-honoured ritual that each family in the village cooked a goose on this particular day, in order to bring good luck for the following 12 months, but several households cooked more than one and donated the additional birds to the airfield kitchen.

No-one mentioned anything about me and the lodger. It seemed Mr Luckett had kept our encounter confidential, and I said nothing to anyone. Life was able to resume as normal, apart from the war, of course, and as winter neared my church organised a two-day walking trip to Snowdonia for the women of the village to celebrate the change of seasons. Joan agreed to assume responsibility for the canteen while I was away, so I looked forward to a brief hiking holiday in north Wales.

CHAPTER 6

THE TWO-DAY VISIT to Snowdonia was the only time each year when the ladies of the village escaped their homes for a little bit of fun. Not every woman went, for fear of what might happen while they were absent, but for others it was an opportunity to get away from the routine of work and wartime rationing. Consequently, this outing was my first chance to meet the other members of the village community since moving back to stay with my parents. During September 1942, when the outing last took place, I was working in Leeds and could not participate; in both 1940 and 1941, the outings were cancelled because of fears of a German invasion. The holiday involved a one-day bus journey, an overnight stay and two-thirds of a day hiking, and we returned home during the evening of the second day.

Our destination was 130 miles (210 km) away in a place called Llanberis in north Wales. The town was to be our base, and each of us would lodge in accommodation provided by members of the congregation of the Llanberis Church in Wales. The area was located at the foot of a spectacular mountain pass and, in part, our visit was to enjoy the autumn foliage that created a beautiful landscape of vivid greens, golds and reds.

Should we arrive in Llanberis early enough, a visit to Dolbadarn Castle was planned. This is a fortification overlooking the pass, and it was built by Llwelyn the Great during the early thirteenth century. It is famous for its round tower and strategic situation, but despite its situation, it was seized and held by the English from 1282.

The arrangement for the following morning was to hike along the Llanberis Path, and most of us hoped to make it as close to the summit of Mount Snowdon as possible without disobeying wartime military restrictions. The mountain was approximately 3,500 feet (1,065 metres) high, and everyone hoped the weather would be kind to us. The path was lengthy, but it rose gently in most places to give easy access to the mountain. We were told that, wherever we had reached by lunchtime, we had to begin our return. Along the route, there were slate quarries and grey slate cottages, and also the Snowdonia Mountain Railway which, although the steam train ran twice a day, was no longer carrying civilian passengers.

To begin the journey to Llanberis, we were asked to congregate on the village green at 10:30am, where the bus would collect us. I was excited to be taking a break from work and spending time in the fresh air, as for the last few days I had felt tired and experienced occasional mild headaches.

The bus was a few minutes late, because it collected people in other villages before reaching ours, and altogether there were about two dozen women on the coach.

We were thankful that the owner of the bus service had chosen to provide for this trip one of his single-decker, green-coloured Leyland 'Tigers'. The vehicle had once had a cream roof, but this had been painted green to camouflage it from the prying eyes of German pilots who might be flying over England and looking for something to attack. The colour made it difficult for the Germans to spot us at night, and during the day we could pull onto the roadside's grassy verge and wait there until the risk of an assault was over.

I climbed aboard and found myself sitting next to a woman who turned out to be Maude, the older sister of Joan Sykes, and we were no sooner in our seats and on the way to north Wales than she started to talk.

After briefly introducing ourselves, she asked if I liked my job and if I was missing living in a big city like Leeds. She told me her sister enjoyed working for me, although she thought me very young for the level of my responsibilities. She complimented my mother on taking care of the lodger, and I acknowledged her comment without disclosing my opinions of the man.

I told her I was happy to be back at home and that the new job was similar to the one I had in Leeds, except much smaller in scope. I complimented her sister on her hard work and how I enjoyed working with her, and then Maude resumed her questioning.

"Don't you miss living in a big city?" she queried. "It has to be so quiet here by comparison."

I agreed but added, "I'm happy that the work here is not as demanding as it was in Leeds. Now I have the time to go dancing with my sister and friends."

"But what about the boys you knew in Leeds? Don't you miss them?" Maude smiled. Really, it was none of her business, but I answered nonetheless, "My boyfriend's away fighting and I'm waiting for him to come home. Even if I had wanted to, I had no time to go out with anyone in Leeds."

"And what type of work did you do there?" Maude's curiosity continued.

I explained how the canteen I managed served several thousand people daily, and that all these people were receiving job training in preparation for supporting the war effort. They came from everywhere, including outside of Britain. There were a number of coloured people who had come from Jamaica and other places, and were the hardest working people I had ever met.

Maude wanted to know more, so I explained.

"They are very friendly people and often their English is better than mine. Most of them volunteered to work in factories for the first time in their lives. On one occasion, a group of eighty came to be trained as machine operators in a munitions works, and during their sixteen weeks' training, none of them missed a day."

"Did you ever hear from them after they were trained?" asked Maude, interested because she had never socialised with people from other countries.

"Oh yes, often. Some returned for more training, and others had friends working at the Institute."

"Did they tell you about the places they came from?"

"Sometimes. Some came from islands like Trinidad and the Bahamas, and others were from South American countries like Guyana and British Honduras. Leeds was a whole new world for them, and both men and women volunteered to help us beat the Germans."

"But why is it so important for them?" I could sense that Maude was a little confused.

"They believed their homes would be attacked by the Germans once Germany had conquered Britain, because Germany would need to use their countries as bases to attack the United States. Therefore, they thought it was better to stop the Germans now, rather than later. Some had menfolk serving in the RAF, and there were lots of stories about mixing with the English. They found it strange going to the pictures and dances where white people were also present, and they hated the weather."

We then talked about our holiday in Llanberis. Neither of us knew much about north Wales, but Maude thought her visit would be a little sad. Apparently, the family with whom she would be staying had lost a 22-year-old family member during a recent bombing raid into Germany. His aircraft had been shot down by a fighter 'plane, and he had been killed in the crash. Several of his colleagues had survived and been made prisoners-of-war.

Soon we were in Llanberis and were met by our hosts near the church. On the way into town, mention was made of a huge underground bomb storage facility in abandoned slate quarries on the edge of town that supplied the Royal Air Force with about 20 percent of its munition needs. Bombs and incendiaries arrived by rail for storage, and they were taken away either by train or by road when needed. A few months earlier, a roof on one of the quarries had collapsed burying 14,000 tons of explosives. We were told not to mention the complex to anyone, and reassured that the site was relatively secure from attack because slate waste had been spread across the area to camouflage it from German aircraft.

Once our personal belongings had been unloaded, those who wanted to went off to view the castle. I was tired so I stayed behind with my host family. The arrangements for the following day were to meet the bus near the railway station at 7:30am and then drive up to the start of the hiking path. We were told that everyone needed to be back in town by 4pm for the departure home.

The Welsh weather chose to be kind on the second day, with a blue sky and fluffy white clouds. In the distance, as we began our climb, we could see the mountain. The only person missing was Florence, the church organist, who sent a message announcing that she preferred not to hike. She and the friend with whom she was staying had decided they were cooks, not hikers, so they would spend the day together preparing traditional recipes from their respective parts of the country. Florence would show her friend how to make Yorkshire pudding, and in return her friend would demonstrate how to prepare Welsh leek soup.

The rest of us left to begin our ascent of Snowdon, and on the way we heard about another of the slate quarries in the area which was rumoured to contain the art collections from the London National and Tate galleries. The galleries' collections were eventually moved from several dispersed Welsh locations to be consolidated deep in a labyrinth of caves in the centre of Snowdonia, and they would stay there for the remainder of the war. Cold, damp caves were not ideal places to store priceless works of art, so before the transfer, several airtight, climate-controlled brick huts had been built to hold them right inside the mountain.

Exactly how high up the mountain we could reach depended on the weather, since the mountain was often covered in mist and cloud. There were steep drops, uneven paths and masses of scree that could cause serious falls down the side of the mountain. If we were lucky, we hoped to complete the 4.5-mile (7.2-km) hike in under 4 hours, but we had to remember that, whatever height we had reached by lunchtime, we would need to walk down again to be ready for the bus to depart at 4pm.

At first, it was a fairly easy walk, although most of us were out of breath and had to keep stopping for a rest. A little over two miles into the hike, I felt terribly exhausted and my shortage of breath worsened. I did not want to embarrass myself in front of my companions, so I struggled onwards until finally I tripped on the rough pathway and fell, scraping my knees.

The injuries were not very painful, but the group was concerned about my well-being if I continued upwards. Several members helped me back to my feet, and I apologised by saying that I was over-stressed from working; I also said that the altitude was affecting me and making me feel sick. Two ladies volunteered to take me back to town, and I gratefully accepted their invitation. We retraced our footsteps, although I do not remember much about the walk, and my companions went somewhere to buy me a cup of tea at the end of the walk, which I drank while they went to collect my belongings to prepare for the bus ride home. They suggested that I should eat something, but I was not hungry.

I felt uncomfortable and embarrassed during the long journey home, as everyone knew I had been sick on the mountainside. The bus had no toilet, which added to my discomfort, and I could feel my feet swelling. Maude sat next to me to make sure that I was okay, and this time she said very little as I periodically tried to sleep. I was exhausted by the time we arrived back in our village, so she walked me home and told my mother what had happened. I said I was feeling much better and my mother should not worry, but she told me to go to bed and she would call the doctor the following morning. Meanwhile, she said I should not go to work, and she asked Maude to let her sister know that I would not return to the airfield until I was fully recovered.

In the morning, I still felt listless and sick. The doctor arrived early, and my mother explained what had happened and how previously I had suffered from exhaustion in Leeds. He carried out a thorough examination, took my temperature, checked my heart-beat, examined my body and asked for a urine sample which he took away. Later in the day, my mother visited his office to find out what was happening and what treatment I should receive. When she arrived home, she came to my bedroom looking very, very upset.

"Do you know what's wrong with you?" she asked angrily. "Have you any idea?"

I really did not have an answer. Other than feeling nauseous during the hike and journey home, everything seemed normal.

"You're pregnant, that's what's wrong with you. What in the world have you been up to? Who was he?" my mother demanded to know.

Her accusation horrified me. It was not what I expected. Suddenly, memories of that evening six weeks ago came racing back. This was the last thing I expected, and although I had missed a period, it had not caused me any concern at the time as it was quite normal. Therefore, I was ill-prepared to defend myself and did not know what to say so I began to weep.

"That won't help," my mother said furiously. "How could you do such a thing? Can you imagine what the villagers will say when they find out? I'll be ashamed to show my face. Wait here until I find your father."

She went, leaving me feeling shocked and very vulnerable. I began to think about the answers to her questions and realised that, if I accused the lodger, he might reject my story and then it would be his word against mine. Even if he did admit to what he had done, he would very likely claim that I had acted willingly, that I had not resisted but gone into his bedroom wearing only a towel. After all, Mr Luckett was a highly respected person in the community, so why would the words of a 20-year-old woman be believed over his? I lay in bed shaking with fear over what was about to happen.

CHAPTER 7

My father trailed into the house behind my mother, looking in disbelief at what he had just been told. By now, I was downstairs waiting in the kitchen for their arrival, and I had decided that it would be better to tell both my parents at the same time, so they would hear the same story, although I remained confused over what might convince them to believe my explanation.

Both my parents could be intimidating. My mother was petite and wore her hair tight to her thin face, was proud of her family's reputation, regularly attended church, set high social standards and expected her daughters to fulfill her expectations. My father was more tolerant and avoided conflict as much as he could; he would either distance himself, if he could not support one side of an argument, or he would be protective if he thought his wife was being overly zealous with her discipline. He was a little taller than my mother, his hair was thinning and turning grey, and he had become rather corpulent.

"Why don't you make us some tea," he patiently asked my mother, "and then we can get to the bottom of this."

A few minutes later, we all took our cups of tea to the more comfortable seating in the front room, and there my mother assertively bid me to explain what had happened.

"You've brought shame on all of us," she complained, "and probably ruined your own life by being so stupid and irresponsible. How could this happen? The entire village will be talking about you after what happened in Snowdonia."

I had not anticipated my mother's unfriendly reaction, which made me feel even more ashamed and embarrassed. My reaction was to cry, but this response received very little sympathy, except from my father who looked at me with heavy eyes.

I tearfully started to explain.

"It's not my fault," I plaintively argued. "It didn't happen because of me, and I never expected to become pregnant. Why would I want that to happen? I have a career to think about and a boyfriend fighting in the war. I'm as upset as you are."

I found sufficient self-confidence to begin my explanation. "It was the lodger, and he assaulted me in his bedroom. I know you won't believe it, but it's true. I was scared to tell you when it happened, but I never thought I'd become pregnant. You regard him as so important that I thought you would scoff at my story."

I described in detail what had taken place, although it hurt to talk about the experience and I doubted that my parents trusted my account. There was still a possibility that the lodger would deny that anything had taken place, and I could not offer any proof to the contrary.

Judging by their looks, both of them were skeptical. Why had I not spoken up at the time if it was not my fault? I repeated that I never expected to become pregnant, but they remained doubtful. It was my mother who responded first.

"We'll find out if any of this is true this evening when Mr Luckett returns," she said. "We'll hear what he has to say, but it's hard to believe he would do such a thing."

It was difficult for my mother to believe that anyone of whom she was so proud could behave in this way, and I was annoyed that she was less worried about my personal situation than she was about the affect my condition would have on her reputation in the village and at the local church.

"I'm telling the truth," I yelled, hoping I could force my parents to accept my story. It did not work.

My mother's final words were: "In that case, you'll have to give up your job, and I don't want you living here while you're pregnant, otherwise people in the village will talk about you. You may not tell anyone what has happened until we decide what to do. Is that understood?"

I nodded, and I was instructed to return to my bedroom and stay there. Under no circumstances should I leave the house. I lay on my bed and wept.

* * *

As soon as Mr Luckett returned, my father invited him into the front room saying there was something important to discuss. I was asked to come downstairs and join the discussion, and it fell to my father to describe what I had told my parents earlier in the day, then ask the lodger if the story was true. He clearly was not expecting the accusation and at first did not seem to know how to respond. He looked at me to gauge my reaction, but I looked away. Was he about to deny the accusation? I waited.

With some reluctance, he admitted that the event had taken place, but it had been consensual. His explanation was that he had had a particularly difficult day at work on that occasion, he had been refused permission to visit his wife and children and I gone into his room wearing only a towel. However, at least he did not deny the assault from ever having taken place, and for that I was relieved.

"She came into my bedroom virtually naked," he firmly insisted. "How more provocative can you get? Maybe I didn't ask, but she didn't resist."

I argued back in my own defence that I had gone into his room only because he asked me to look at a letter he had written, and I was wearing only a towel because I had just had a bath and was about to get dressed to go out dancing. He had been drinking and had offered me a glass of whisky. My protests did not appear to impress my parents, as they could not understand why I would have gone into his room under the circumstance I described. I wanted to say that I did so because he was so important to them and I did not want to upset either him or my parents. However, I thought that such a claim was likely to sound implausible and self-serving.

Mr Luckett became irritated and asked my father what he planned to do.

"I don't want people at work hearing about this accusation because it could affect my job at the airfield," he said.

My father was uncertain what to do, and my mother was concerned that knowledge of the pregnancy should not be made public.

My father replied, "I probably should report the incident to the police, but I'm not sure that will help in the middle of a war. There's little point in harming you and the airfield or embarrassing our daughter publicly."

My mother added that she did not want any third party involved. To her, the lodger was an important person, and to have the police contacted would only worsen the situation and not change anything.

Mr Luckett agreed with the proposal and offered to help me with my expenses during the pregnancy if everything were kept quiet. He was not sure when he would tell his wife, and no-one discussed what would happen once my pregnancy was over.

It had been an extraordinarily stressful day, and I wanted to go away and hide. I retired upstairs to lie on my bed, feeling stressed and emotionally drained, only to experience the return of the nausea. However, if I had to throw up, it was better to do it in the privacy of my own bathroom than elsewhere. Plainly, my mother was shocked by what had happened and had chosen to blame me. I had done "a terrible thing" she later told me. Suddenly my life was shattered into a million pieces, and all my plans for the future were destroyed.

* * *

I wondered if my parents would ask Mr Luckett to leave his lodgings, but they did not. He remained with us, and for several days he and I travelled to the airfield separately. At work I chose to avoid him, and I felt awkward when I saw him at home, but he would usually quickly disappear into his own room. I told Joan Sykes that I was resigning my job due to fatigue, as the doctor had ordered me to take several weeks of rest, and I would probably spend most of this time away from home.

Meanwhile, my mother contacted relatives to find someone who would volunteer to look after me, as she wanted me out of the village as quickly as possible. There was an expectation that my pregnancy would go to full term, because abortions were illegal, but what would happen to the child thereafter was left unaddressed

My parents became very subdued, and while they treated me with respect, their smiles and laughter disappeared. I was left on my own because my older sister moved to the farm where she was a Land Girl, and my younger sister relocated to the village where we used to live in order to sit her school examinations. I felt isolated and blamed myself for what had happened.

In the village, there were whispers about what might be taking place, but only our neighbour knew officially that I was expecting. I was kept indoors so no-one could see me, and although I thought about writing to my boyfriend, I decided to wait.

No-one at the airfield knew what was taking place. George Luckett had apparently kept his word and told no-one, not even Michael Fromm, although he did start discussions to change his lodgings. His superiors agreed to billet him at an airfield a few miles away as soon as they had available accommodation.

One evening, he and I had a private conversation during which he told me that he had not yet told his wife about what had happened, and he asked me whether—when he did, and if she divorced him—I would be willing to marry him. I told him unequivocally that under no circumstances would I consider marriage to him. We had never dated, I very much disliked him after what he had put me through, and I already had a boyfriend. Also, as she had two young children, I asked him why his wife would want a divorce. I pondered his offer and wondered if he hoped that, by marrying me, he would avoid any risk of prosecution should my father change his mind and report the incident to the police because, in Britain, it was not legally possible for a husband to be prosecuted for raping his wife; under the law she was considered as little more than one of his chattels, to be used as he saw fit. We did not talk about what would happen to the baby after it was born, but my mother confirmed that an abortion was out of the question. She said I should arrange for the baby to be adopted as soon as it arrived, and her proposition was non-negotiable.

I was also told that I would not be invited to my older sister's wedding, even though the ceremony would be in the church next to our house, and the reception would take place in our neighbour's barn.

CHAPTER 8

It took only a few days for my mother to get rid of me. I was abandoned, although in hindsight I wonder if she may have had my best interests at heart and was simply trying to protect me from public denouncements and safeguard the reputations of my sisters. Nonetheless, I was devastated that she thought I was the one at fault, and the fact that she took the side of the lodger.

"Where are you sending me?" I asked her one day.

"I don't know yet, but I'm working on it," was her irritated reply.

A couple of days later she arranged for a priority telegram to be sent from the local Post Office to her married sister, who lived in a small village near Scarborough on the east coast of Yorkshire, to ask if she would take care of me. My mother was careful to ask the postmaster to ensure that the telegram did not look like those sent to notify families that a relative had been killed in the war. She was afraid that the telegraph messenger boy, or "angel of death" as they were sometimes nicknamed, would be insensitive and cause her sister to refuse to help if she were frightened by the way the message was delivered. It remained unusual for a household to receive any form of telegram.

My mother considered her elder sister to be the ideal guardian. She had managed a guest house in Scarborough, was respected by the community because she was married to the local policeman, and no-one would know who I was. I was told to take my ration book, and that my aunt would receive a weekly stipend for her services from Mr Luckett.

It did not take long for my mother to finalise the arrangements.

"You're going to stay with your aunt, and on Saturday you and Mr Luckett will drive to her home and he'll give her the weekly allowance for the next two months. You need to do as you are told while living there, and make sure you complete arrangements for the arrival of the baby."

"What do I need to pack?" I asked, immediately acquiescent.

"Everything for the next few months," was her simple reply. "I don't want you living here while you're in this state." She scowled and stared at my tummy.

"Mr Luckett will bring additional clothes if you need them, and he's supposed to help you buy the items you'll need when the child is born. We don't have the resources to purchase your baby things."

* * *

On the way to my aunt's, I learned from Mr Luckett that the allowance was one guinea (one pound and one shilling) a week, and he expected to pay this amount until the baby arrived. My parents had insisted that he drive my car and take it back to them, so they could store it in their garage until I returned, as they did not want me driving away from my aunt's home for any reason.

I had never stayed in my aunt's house before, and I hoped I would be safe from German aircraft that were active in her neighbourhood, as recently they had been machine-gunning nearby stockyards and farms. Also, the York to Scarborough railway line ran close to her property, and there had been reports of German pilots following trains and then machine-gunning and bombing the rail carriages.

Scarborough had suffered similarly from air raids, with everything from incendiaries to parachute land-mines being dropped on the town. However, the town had recently been left alone.

Mr Luckett and I did not do much talking during the journey, although at one point he repeated his offer of matrimony.

"I'm prepared to marry you if you want," he said.

I looked at him in disbelief that he assumed I would be grateful or awed by his offer. I was not.

"Why would I marry you when you're already married and have two children?" I replied. "Yes, I'm carrying your baby, but becoming your wife is the last thing I would want to do after what you did to me. Frankly, I don't like you."

"And what will you do with the baby on your own," he glowered back at me.

"I don't know, but it's none of your business," I retaliated. "I expect you to help me financially, but otherwise you can stay away. What I do with the baby will be my decision, not yours."

I sensed his anger, but our conversation ended, and he stayed silent for the rest of the journey. It was cloudy and cold when we reached our destination, with a bitter east wind blowing in from the North Sea. Both of us were civil towards each other in front of my aunt, and Mr Luckett carried my suitcase into the house. He declined to stay for a cup of tea, however, saying he needed to get back to the airfield, and that was the last time I ever saw him.

My aunt lived in a small village between Malton and Scarborough, in a house that was built of brick, with a red pantile roof. It was a picturesque but quiet rural area, and my parents had told me to stay in the house at all times. The only exception I discovered was that, on some evenings, I was allowed to sit in the garden with my aunt and listen to the formations of British bombers headed east across the coast on their way to bomb Germany.

It was like being a prisoner in jail. My aunt was kind and fed me, but there was nothing much to do. The only entertainment was the British Broadcasting Corporation's Home Service, which we received through an old battery-operated valve radio that crackled and faded in and out while I listened. There were hours of dance music, *It's That Man Again* was one of my aunt's favorite shows, and we also listened to *The Week in Westminster* and *Children's Hour*. I read a lot and mulled over what I should do with the baby.

Occasionally I was permitted to leave the house in the company of my aunt. She would take me to Scarborough to do her weekly shopping, and we would meet her husband who was a policeman there. She grew blackcurrants, gooseberries and damson plums in her garden, and she sold jars of her delicious jam to shopkeepers—presumably on the black market (the illegal trade in scarce commodities).

It was always a slow journey to Scarborough. There were barriers and guards controlling the roads into and out of town, and access to many areas was prohibited because members of the armed forces were billeted there. We passed by bomb-damaged houses and buildings, and while some shops were open in the morning, they closed early in the afternoon because of the blackout regulations. Even the picture houses and dancehalls operated for only a few hours each day. The beaches were protected by rolls of barbed wire, and the fishing fleet was docked in the harbour, although there was always the risk that a trawler would be machine-gunned or bombed by a passing German 'plane, either in port or out at sea.

It was easy to stroll in some of the parks because the wrought iron railings had been removed so that their metal could be melted down and used in the war effort. It was not unusual to see groups of children playing in the parks and walking around the town, as bus-loads of youngsters were periodically brought to live in Scarborough and the surrounding villages from places vulnerable to heavy German bombing, like Hull, Middlesborough and Hartlepool. I was told that about 80 children had arrived from Brighton several months earlier because they were considered to have been living in a front-line town.

My aunt made sure that we left Scarborough before dark, when the compulsory blackout was enforced. It was considered dangerous to be driving or walking during the long, dark nights, even though trees, the kerbs alongside pavements and other obstacles had been painted with white bands for recognition and safety.

There was one occasion when my aunt drove me well south of Scarborough to visit a friend of hers. I was told to pretend to be her niece on holiday, recovering from overwork, and to stay quiet. On the way home we passed a new airfield that was under construction, and I asked if it was for fighters or bombers.

"Both," said my aunt, "although mainly for bomber aircraft. It's supposed to be a FIDO when it opens."

"What's a FIDO?" I asked.

"Well, I'm no expert," she replied, "but I think it's an airfield where damaged 'planes can land if they can't make it back to their base airfield after a raid on Germany or when fog obscures their regular landing strip. It's not open yet, but it will provide emergency landing as part of the country's Fog Investigation and Dispersal Operations."

I later learned that the facility was used by bomber crews in both situations but in particular when it was foggy inland. Large areas of Britain could be simultaneously fog-bound, and earlier in the war this phenomenon had been responsible for a number of aircraft losses. FIDO consisted of two pipelines, situated along either side of a runway, through which fuel could be pumped and then released via burner jets that were set at regular intervals along the pipeline. The runway was wider than normal, and the result when the burner jets were lit was a wall of flame on either side of it that would warm the air and evaporate suspended droplets of fog to create a clearing over the runway. Some airfields had their own FIDO system, but this facility, with its one airstrip, was dedicated to fog dispersal emergencies. By the end of hostilities, 1,600 aircraft had made emergency FIDO landings.

* * *

Just before Christmas there was a knock on the door and my aunt received her second telegram from my mother. The news was not good. The telegram read:

"Our lodger has stopped paying the guinea each week and left our home. Our daughter will pay you until year-end and then we'll collect her on 1st January and bring her back here. More when my husband sees you."

It turned out that Mr Luckett had left his lodgings to live in the accommodation now available at the nearby airfield, but he gave no reason for stopping his payments. While I had a little money saved up from my Leeds work, I could not afford similar payments for the full duration of my pregnancy.

Christmas came and went. There were no gifts and only a handful of decorations placed around the house to remind us of the time of year. At least we had a Christmas dinner, as back in February my aunt had prepared a Christmas pudding (a sweet dessert containing dried fruit), and she exchanged five jars of her jam for a goose from a local farmer. My bulge stayed hidden under my loose-fitting clothes.

On Saturday, 1st January 1944, my father collected me, and as we drove home he asked about my stay. I told him that my aunt had been kind to me, and I was no longer suffering from nausea. I felt rested and relaxed, and I was looking forward to being back with my family.

A few miles later, he broke the silence again.

"You should know that your mother has found you a job in York and wants you out of the house as much as possible. The work is clerical, and you are supposed to start work early Monday morning. She's also talking to relatives about having them adopt the child."

"I'm not sure I want my baby adopted," I replied. "And what type of work has she found me?"

"It's an office job," he replied. "You'll be sitting most of the time, so that's a good thing because of your health, and you can have your car back to get to work."

"How did she find the job?" I wanted to know.

"One of her cousins volunteered to use his work contacts. The job should be fine. You'll leave home early in the morning, when it's dark, and return in the evening after nightfall so that no-one in the village will see you."

I grimaced and repeated my question about adoption.

"The baby's going to be illegitimate," my father replied, "and if you don't have it adopted, it will end up in a children's home. There's no way you can keep it."

I sensed another battle ahead with my parents. I knew they wanted me out of sight of the neighbours, but now a fresh conflict was developing. Our home was private, surrounded by a ten-foot brick wall over which no one could see, and there were large wooden gates at the end of the driveway, so it was impossible to see me once I drove onto our property, but I could see a new struggle ahead of me—one that might prevent my child from ever coming home to be with me.

I fell silent, angry that my mother wanted to control my future. It sounded as if her attitude had not changed, and life would resume its confrontational nature. She might be right about the baby, but I was not ready to make that decision. I was also beginning to think that I needed to take legal action against Mr Luckett to make him pay something towards the cost of supporting his child.

We completed our journey without further conversation. Travel that afternoon was slow because of the rain and cold, and sleet was falling by the time we arrived home. I greeted my mother briefly, then immediately retired to bed, expecting to hear more about the job the following morning.

CHAPTER 9

On Sunday morning, I rose shortly after daybreak, feeling content to have returned home to everything familiar, and busied myself in my bedroom sorting out clothes and preparing a pile of dirties for the wash. I noticed that the room opposite was unoccupied; the door was partially open, and the bed was made, but there were no signs of anyone's personal belongings. Going downstairs, I found my father in the front room, sitting by a warm coal fire. He told me to go to the kitchen and prepare whatever breakfast I wanted, and that my mother and two sisters were at church but would be home soon. As I wandered around the house, nothing seemed to have changed except for the empty bedroom.

Eventually, I sat down with my father and asked about the latest village news. Apparently, there was very little new gossip. Most people did not know about my pregnancy, and the airfield had not yet opened, although it was nearly complete and the assigned squadron was expected to move there within a few weeks.

"Where's the lodger?" I felt confident enough to ask.

"We don't know," replied my father as he shook his head. "Apparently he's still working here but living elsewhere. Your sister's husband-to-be lives close to the girl who's dating the American, and he heard that he's helping out with other airfields. Supposedly, he has been given permission to go and see his family."

* * *

When my mother returned, she announced that it was no longer raining and the weather for the time being was pleasantly mild. Since my father's Sunday plans were to clean out the greenhouse and do some preparation for planting vegetables, he welcomed the news and went into the garden. My two sisters had disappeared, so my mother removed her coat and hat, sat down, gave me a solemn look and then started to explain my new job.

"It's work in an accounts office in York, and you'll be employed as a book-keeper," she told me. "Office hours are 8.30am to 6.30pm, and you report to someone called Dot Daniels. Be thankful that I have relatives who are willing to find you a job. You should be out of the house before daylight, and don't return home until after dark."

I knew she did not want me to be seen by the villagers, so although office work was frowned upon by the people I knew, because they thought it required no skills and needed little knowledge, it was clear that I could not resume my former type of work. It was equally clear that there was no point in arguing.

"And have you decided about the baby?" my mother challenged. "Your dad and I want it adopted, and you need to make a decision quickly. There are new rules that require babies to be adopted within fourteen days of birth, and once the child has a new home, you can't claim it back; also, the placement has to be managed by an authorised adoption agency."

"But it has to be my decision" I argued back. "I'm its mother, so I should decide what happens to the baby."

"We'll sort that out later," was my mother's stern reaction, and she continued, "It's not just what you want. What you've done involves the whole family and, fortunately, I've found a cousin interested in taking your child. They want their own children, but I've told them they can start their family by adopting your baby."

I was disgusted by the idea, but it was the sort of thing that my mother would do. When I was small, I spent most of my school holidays with an aunt and an uncle who was my mother's youngest brother. They had no children of their own, and the original plan was that I should live with them on a permanent basis, as such agreements were quite normal among families back before World War II. However, I had apparently been so unhappy with the arrangement that my parents brought me home.

Later that day, I had an opportunity to talk to my older sister. She sympathised with my condition and appeared to be the only family member who believed in my version of what happened. She was sorry that I would be unable to attend her wedding but said that, once she was married, I would always be welcome to visit her and her husband, as they would be living on a farm only a few miles away. She asked about my health, and what it felt like to carry a baby, and she wanted to hear about my time with my aunt.

She also mentioned that construction at the airfield was virtually complete, but bad weather during December had caused last-minute delays. Aircraft and flight personnel would start arriving at the beginning of April and would be housed in Nissan huts erected in the village. Joan Sykes continued to manage the canteen.

I was surprised when she asked, "Have you heard about our former lodger being promoted?"

"I hope not," I replied. "What happened?"

She said she had a long conversation with Joan Sykes and, apparently, Number 4 Bomber Command wanted someone to take charge of planning repairs and upgrades for all of its airfields, so that the number of bombing raids could be maximised, and Mr Luckett was given the task. In appreciation of his work, the authorities had approved his home leave to visit his family. She had heard that both his children were in good health and that his wife was an opera singer, and before the war, she had almost turned professional.

My sister paused a moment, but before I could ask more questions about Mr Luckett, she switched to a more serious topic.

"Our mother is still very angry with you. She blames you for what happened, and wants the baby adopted and placed as far away from here as possible. She's really very upset."

I told my sister that I did not think I wanted to give up the child. I had not asked to become pregnant, but it was my life that was being altered, and therefore I thought it should be up to me to determine the baby's future.

* * *

I rose early on Monday morning, while it was still dark outside, as on the way to work I had to cross the River Derwent, which was notorious for flooding. With overcast skies and rain the previous week, I worried that there might be delays, but my anxiety was unjustified since the amount of rain that had fallen was insufficient to cause flooding, and my journey was uneventful.

The office turned out to be in a cold, damp concrete building located next to a factory, and I quickly discovered that I needed to wear an overcoat and a neck-scarf to keep warm. I occasionally required gloves, too, although they messed up my efficiency.

That first morning, I reported to my supervisor and gave her my employment details. She needed my name, address, age (then 21), tax details and the names of my next of kin. I was shown to my desk, instructed how to complete office paperwork and introduced to the department's filing system. It was simple work that I learned quickly. Dot was easy to talk to, had an engaging sense of humor and very quickly realised that I was pregnant by the clothes I was wearing, my frequent visits to the bathroom and the manner of my walk.

She was probably in her late-40s, was a little taller than my mother, had a forever smiling face and had a little weight around her waist and upper arms. She wore utility clothing, and her short, tight curls were permed to stay away from her face.

One particularly bitter winter's evening shortly after I arrived, she invited me to her terraced home to meet her husband and stay overnight, rather than drive home in the cold. They had no children, and her husband had been made redundant from the railways after injuring his back. Their home was an unpretentious two-up/two-down, brick-built house, with the front door opening directly onto the street from the living room, and the kitchen facing a back-walled garden that included an outdoor toilet. The reason for her invitation was never made explicit, but I suspected that she saw me as a surrogate daughter, so if my mother wanted me out of her house, Dot was willing to offer me her own home as a substitute.

I quickly grew to like Dot. She cared for her staff, and one evening she stopped by my desk to remark how my bump was pushing its way beneath my dress. She asked about my circumstances, and I possibly told her more than I should. I described the relationship with Mr Luckett, his importance in the local community, and how my mother had not forgiven me for what happened. Dot believed that my choice regarding the future of my baby was the most important decision I would ever take in my life. Although she sympathised with the wishes of my parents, she believed that, whatever I decided, I must feel that I had done the right thing for my child. The decision should be governed by the needs of the baby, not by some selfish wish on the part of myself or my parents.

She asked for details about the baby's father, so I told her that he was married with two children, and that he was refusing to provide me with any form of financial support, so I was very much on my own. Dot was outraged and immediately arranged for me to see a solicitor to discuss taking legal action to claim child maintenance. She wanted us to have lunch together later in the week to talk more about my situation.

We ate at one of the civic restaurants that had opened up during wartime to feed members of the public who otherwise would not have had access to hot food because of bomb damage to their homes. The menu was limited, but the price of the meal was well below the five shillings maximum that restaurants were permitted to charge. During the meal, Dot asked me about medical care, and I told her that my mother preferred me not to use the family doctor. Instantly, she volunteered to ask her own general practitioner to take care of me, and by the end of January I was being examined monthly by Dot's doctor. There was no National Health Service then, so I had to pay, but the charges were nominal.

I do not know why Dot befriended me so kindly; she had no relationship with my family, but she permanently lavished affection on me. Her city upbringing was very different from my countryside background, but it was as if she wanted to adopt me so that she could shower me with acts of kindness whenever she had the chance. Maybe I was a substitute for the children that she had never had but, anyway, our friendship was to last for many years. After my baby was born, I was welcome to take it to her home whenever my child needed feeding.

She asked me what I had bought for the baby, and I told her nothing.

"Let me help you," she implored. "We can shop together during lunch breaks."

I thanked her and agreed that would be helpful. She also asked about maternity clothes, because she could see that my bump was beginning to win the battle with my regular clothes, so I told her I had none.

"You should keep a list of everything you buy," she stressed, "and keep receipts for everything. That way the solicitor can use the list when he submits claims for child support."

I told her I would keep a note of everything as soon as we started shopping.

Then she said something which came as a great surprise to me.

"I worry that you are starting your third trimester and still driving long distances to work," Dot said. "Anything could happen when you are miles from anywhere, and I'd never forgive myself if something dreadful happened to you. Why don't you move in and live with us for the next few weeks? We have a spare bedroom. That way you and I can go shopping and it will be easier for you to continue work."

I was stunned by such a kind offer and told my parents about the invitation. They accepted Dot's proposal immediately, and in mid-February I moved in to live with her and her husband. It was up to me whether or not I returned home at weekends, but since my parents were normally busy, I stayed at Dot's until the doctor told me to stop work and stay at home.

During this period, Dot did everything to help me prepare for my baby's arrival, including accompanying me to my monthly doctor's visits and giving me advice about my meetings with the solicitor. I was told that the baby's father had financial obligations and the solicitor would file a claim with the relevant magistrates' court. The claim would cover all expenses incurred during my pregnancy, as well as financial support for my child until it was aged 15 and able to leave school. This gave me hope that I could keep my baby and would not have to accede to my parents' wishes.

Much to my surprise, Dot and I had great fun when we went shopping together. I was starting to move about slowly, but Dot was patient with me. We bought lots of things, and I recorded the price of each item, including:

Cot and Mattress	2 pounds, 19 shillings, 9 pence
Pram	8 pounds, 6 shillings, 6 pence
Nappies	1 pound, 16 shillings, 0 pence
Baby clothes	1 pound, 9 shillings, 9 pence
Name tags	6 shillings, 0 pence

I also bought some maternity clothes, the doctor needed to be paid for my examinations, and the fee charged by the solicitor was significant. Therefore, my list of purchases soon totaled in excess of 70 pounds sterling and my savings were disappearing fast. When I left Dot's home in mid-April to resume living with my parents, she told me that I was welcome to return to live with her and her husband at any time, even after the baby arrived.

"You should know that you and your baby will always be welcome here," said the kindly soul, "and I'll do whatever I can to help you."

Dot was not a blood relative, but a friend I found purely by accident, yet she seemed driven to do all she could to help me. Perhaps it was because she was a keen churchgoer and took seriously the business of being truly Christian.

* * *

Once back home with my parents, I decided I should write to my mother's cousin in Leeds and also show courage by writing to my boyfriend overseas, although I did not know where his tank regiment might be stationed. I also decided to write to my aunt in Scarborough as soon as the baby arrived, as I had promised to tell her whether it was a boy or a girl.

My older sister talked to me on several occasions about my plans for the baby. I had not made a final decision at that stage, but my inclination was to keep the baby—much to my mother's annoyance—in the expectation that the court would order Mr Luckett to pay child support. The more the baby kicked inside me, the more maternal I became. I heard from my sister that construction of the airfield was complete, and that the main body of aircraft and flight crews had moved in during mid-April. The squadron was expected to be fully operational and flying bombing missions sometime in May. She said it was amazing to see the huge and noisy 'Halifax' bombers close up. Nothing new had been heard about Mr Luckett, and his American friend was believed to be looking for something else to do in Yorkshire so that he could stay close to his girlfriend.

* * *

My father felt anxious whenever I was in the garden with him. My shortness of breath and early-warning contractions had him scrambling to prepare his car in readiness to take me to the New Earswick (near York) Maternity Hospital. What I would do with the baby was still not finalised, but he did not want me to worry, and he wanted me to be happy. It came down to a choice between early adoption or keeping the baby, as no-one wanted the child sent to a government home, or for both of us to be moved into a mother-and-baby hostel. If necessary, I thought I could pretend to be a war widow and move in with Dot and her husband, and no-one would ever know that my child was illegitimate; it would be assumed that my husband was killed during the war. My own instincts and Dot's kind offer, together with the belief that I would receive financial support from the baby's father, made me strongly inclined to keep my child.

* * *

It was one of those warm, sunny spring days when my baby decided to arrive. I was in the garden late in the evening, helping my father weed the strawberries. The weeds had flourished, thanks to the April and early May showers, but I suddenly felt severe and repeated contractions and told my father. There was no hesitation. He pushed me into the back seat of the car and we were on our way to the maternity hospital through the narrow country roads of the East Riding of Yorkshire that were so familiar to me. We did not think of German bombers wishing to harm us; he just drove as quickly as he could.

Two hours after admission, and early the following morning, I delivered a perfect son. As the child cried, I could hear in the background an Italian tenor singing *Ave Maria* (Hail, Mary) accompanied by a violinist. I took this as a very personal message from God to me: "Blessed art thou among women, and blessed is the fruit of your womb." As a Christian I respected the Bible story in Luke 1:28 about the angel Gabriel greeting the Blessed Virgin Mary and telling her that she will be overcome by the Holy Spirit and bear a son. I have to admit that, for many years thereafter, whenever I heard this melody I stopped whatever I was doing to listen and pray, as it was the final spur that finalised my decision to keep my child. Even though I had been banned from attending church during my pregnancy, I really felt that God had given me a direction.

I was relieved that my baby was healthy, and I instantly fell in love with his blonde hair and blue eyes. Surely, I had been given the child for a purpose that did not include giving him up for adoption? The shame of my body being violated was replaced by an exhilarating feeling of wanting to nurture and take care of my child. Illegitimate or not, I decided that I would never sacrifice the life of my baby son to someone else.

My sense of contentment remained as I lay there cuddling my baby close.

For the next few days, my father visited on most days, and Dot came to the hospital whenever she could. On one occasion, she brought with her a bag of used baby clothes that she said a neighbour had donated to me, as the neighbour had given birth to a son six months earlier.

My older sister visited each day and I shared my secrets with her.

She agreed to help me take care of my baby whenever I needed it, and she also mentioned that successful bombing missions had begun from the airfield.

I stayed relaxed throughout the rest of my stay in the hospital, and I chose to call my baby John.

"Why John?" inquired my father. It was not a family name, but he was delighted that at long last there was a male child in the family that would carry his surname.

"Because of John Bull," I replied, "but don't worry; he has yours as his second name."

John Bull was Britain's national mascot during the war, and I had seen many images of him on posters. I thought of my son as an accident of war, and therefore the name seemed appropriate.

"His is the character of Britain, so the name acknowledges my determination, as well as that of the country, never to accept defeat," I said.

The peace and quiet of the maternity hospital came to an end when I returned to my parents' home. The arguments with my mother developed into a family feud when I insisted on keeping my child, and I threatened to move back to Dot's if she kept insisting on adoption. My father persuaded my mother to give her daughter a little more time to finalise a decision, and then everything became unimportant because of D-Day. Bombers from the airfield were busy attacking rail junctions and marshalling yards, and everyone was looking forward to the liberation of France.

I had written several letters during my final weeks of pregnancy, and I had time to pen a couple more after John arrived. Soon I began to receive replies, and they caused me a mixture of hope and sadness.

The aunt near Scarborough with whom I had spent time wrote back with words of encouragement:

> "Thank you for your most interesting letter. It was wise to write and tell your friends. I think you will be more your own mistress if you live with your friend (Dot), don't you? I would love to see John, but I don't know when."

The words from my cousin who lived in Leeds were discouraging:

"Many thanks for your letter. We were wondering what had happened to you. I think you will be foolish not to follow your family's wishes. It will be better in the long run for both you and the child. If you have the child adopted by some nice people, it will take their name and need never know it was illegitimate. Also, it perhaps will have a better chance than you can give it."

However, the letter that was the most difficult to read came from my boyfriend, still assigned to his tank troop somewhere in Europe:

"Thank you for your letter, which I received today. To tell you the truth, I haven't got over the shock of the news yet. I have read your letter seven or eight times since tea. You say in your letter that if you don't hear from me you will understand. Well, as you see, I have written to you as soon as I could. I must say your letter has altered my plans for when I return home. Needless to say, I am a very disappointed soldier tonight."

I also wrote to tell Mr Luckett that he now had a second son, but I did not have his home address, so instead I posted the letter to him c/o Bomber Command, but I never received a reply.

All this family turmoil occurred around the date of the Allied invasion of Europe on 6th June 1944, and simultaneously my mother announced that she wanted to attend a church service on the other side of York to commemorate the death of her best friend, Mrs Savage, who had lived on a farm in the middle of nowhere and died of cancer a short time earlier. The service was to take place close to where we used to farm before the war, and I was asked to drive my mother to church and pay my respects to her friend because she was someone I also knew well; I had spent a lot of time with her as a child growing up, and I had sat beside her in church for many years. It was arranged that my older sister would accompany us, to help look after the baby, but I had no idea that my mother had a hidden purpose for wanting me to be there.

CHAPTER 10

THE DRIVE TOOK a little over an hour, often along narrow country lanes that only days earlier had swarmed with military vehicles and armed forces personnel. Now, soldiers and troop carriers had gone to support the invasion of Europe, and civilian traffic was relatively light. It was a different matter in the skies. Aircraft were leaving and returning from missions over Europe to the point that we could see queues of 'planes waiting to land.

The airfield that was constructed adjacent to the church during 1940 had been converted into a fully-equipped heavy bomber station, with hard runways replacing the small grassy airfield that had been home to 'Spitfires'. The slit-trench defences constructed when the facility was first opened were still present, although the threat of invading German parachutists had faded. In order to locate the landing site, pilots used as navigation points York Minster to the north, the York to Selby railway line to the west, and the river Ouse on the south-east side—that was when it could be seen, as fog often rolled in off the river, especially during early mornings, sometimes causing flying accidents.

Pilots operating from other airfields nearby also sometimes made mistakes. One tried to land his aircraft on a road alongside an airfield, mistaking it for the main runway. The 'plane crashed, destroying 20 houses. Another pilot overshot the runway and crashed into a farm house, killing the owners and their eldest son who were in bed at the time.

* * *

My mother had a strong association with the Savage family. She had gone to school with Henry Savage's wife, and they had jointly participated in the village's branch of the Women's Institute (WI). Together they attended the monthly all-women meetings of the WI and helped establish their branch's agenda of activities, which focused on education, information and home-based enterprises such as cooking, rug making, sewing, knitting and fund raising. The Savages had no children of their own, and as a young child I had regularly helped Mrs Savage around the house and often stayed on their farm overnight. My first boyfriend was one of their farmhands, although the relationship did not last very long. He took me to the pictures in York for the first time in my life, but I do not think my mother was enthusiastic about the relationship.

Unfortunately, Henry Savage's wife had contracted cancer just before I left for Leeds, and the couple had sold up and moved to a farm on a bleak and inhospitable moor a few miles away. Occasionally, I called in on them during my visits from Leeds to see my parents.

The drive to the church service for my mother's friend was not a particularly pleasant one, as my mother continued to debate the future of my baby, this time in front of my sister. Her opinions were as strong as ever that I should have the baby adopted and resume my career. She also threatened that, if I did not give up the baby, I could not live with her. What she did not know was that Dot Daniels had already invited me to move in with her and her husband once the baby arrived, if I was still unwelcome at home, and Dot's doctor was still taking care of me and my son.

* * *

The memorial service was a sad affair, with the church full of friends from the village that the Savages had known before they moved. I heard that Mr Savage was being looked after by a sister because he had been diagnosed with diabetes and took insulin to stabilise his condition. Unfortunately, the amount of insulin necessary for him to take was difficult to determine because farming was such physical work that his condition could vary dramatically from day to day; if he took too much, he could become dizzy, confused and irritable; if he took too little, he could fall into a diabetic coma. As a result, he and his sister often argued, and she wanted to return to her own home as soon as possible. He employed a local woman to come in each day to clean the house, do his laundry and bake for him, but she could not supervise his medical condition.

The congregation assembled in a small stone church that dated back to the fourteenth century and stood by a field grazed by sheep. I parked my car, left my sister in the car with my baby and walked about a quarter of a mile to the churchyard. Behind the church flowed the wide and slow-moving river Ouse, the same river which created the fog that interfered with the flight operations at the nearby airfield.

Once the service was over, my mother and I chatted with Mr Savage who was pleased to see us at the service. He also seemed glad to see me, and he had not changed much since I last saw him. He stood about six feet tall with thinning grey hair and a gaunt-looking face, and his physique was lean except for rough hands and thick forearms. I was introduced to his sister and some of his other relatives, and then he gave me an invitation.

"You should come over and see me one of these days, and bring your baby with you," he smiled, then turned his attention to his other guests before I had time to respond. We returned to the car, and on the way home my mother made an unexpected proposal.

"Mr Savage's sister says she can't look after her brother any longer, and Mr Savage wonders if you would like the job. You would live with him, and he's offered to pay you a wage, so you can restart your life and have the baby adopted."

I was astonished at the proposal, and at the same time alarmed once more at the thought of losing my child.

"Under no circumstances will I give up my baby," I argued back, "and I don't need the money. The Court is likely to order Mr Luckett to pay me child support, according to my solicitor, and there's a hearing on my petition arranged for 19th August 1944. Meanwhile, if I have to, I will move in with Dot Daniels."

My sister tried to bring calm to our conversation. "I'll take care of the baby if you at least want to try out the job," she said.

I told her it was not necessary. On no account would I give up my child, and the thought of living on an isolated farm did not excite me. The farm was at least a mile from any village, and the only other human companionship in the area were the people living in the farm on the opposite side of the road.

My mother remained silent for the rest of the journey, and afterwards I stayed out of her way. For a couple of days I had a slight cold and worried that I would infect my baby, but it did not happen—presumably because I was breast-feeding him.

As my cold disappeared, the situation with Mr Savage altered. My mother announced that he was happy for me to take my baby, and he would still pay me a weekly wage, as his sister was eager to return home. Given that life at home was so stressful, and most nights I was kept awake by departing and returning bomber aircraft, I reluctantly agreed to the proposal. Dot Daniels assured me that the invitation to live with her and her husband was still available, and I was welcome to visit her whenever I wanted.

I was asked by my father not to take the car, but use my bicycle instead, as I would have access to Mr Savage's vehicle. Two days later, Mr Savage arrived at my parents' home to collect me and my baby, and after a one-hour journey, my life on a moorland farm began. He said that his sister had already departed, he would continue to use his daily help, and he was happy for Dot Daniels to visit me. He also said he knew that I was processing through the courts a claim for Mr Luckett to pay me child support.

To me then, the fighting in Europe seemed a long way away. However, we heard that Florence in Italy had just been liberated by the Allies, the French Resistance had begun an uprising leading to the freedom of Paris, the Allies had entered Belgium, and that 30,000 rail workers in the Netherlands were on strike and had gone into hiding from the Nazis on instructions from the Dutch government-in-exile operating out of London.

* * *

The work looking after Mr Savage was hard, but I was treated well. The farm was mainly grassland used for rearing cattle, sheep and lambs, and there was also a sty and pens for pigs, several sheds for raising calves and a stockyard for cows. Two horses were kept to pull the machinery needed for planting and harvesting a single field of wheat, and I had the task of caring for the poultry as well as looking after the health of my host.

Daily, I received domestic help from a woman who pedaled two miles each way from one of the local villages, who worked from 9am to 4pm and was paid a small weekly wage, plus given free milk and potatoes. Monday was washing day, on Tuesday she baked, on Wednesday she cleaned upstairs, on Thursday we both looked after the house while Mr Savage attended York cattle market, and on Friday the whole house was cleaned, including windows, brasses and kitchen silverware. Gradually we developed a Thursday tradition whereby I would accompany Mr Savage on his journey to the livestock market, but my baby and I would be dropped off at Dot Daniel's house, and he would collect us on his way home. If for any reason Dot was going to be out on a Thursday, she would write to me in advance and I would stay at the farm.

The two-storey, brick-built farmhouse had three bedrooms upstairs, and a kitchen, parlour, dining-room and sitting-room downstairs. The house was attached to the farm outbuildings which included an outside toilet and a laundry copper. The latter was a small, square unit built of bricks and inside it stood a coal furnace. The fire heated a large metal bucket, into which dirty laundry was placed and boiled, and then transferred to a peggy tub where it was churned manually with a washing dolly, and the clothes were finally hung outside to dry after the water had been squeezed out of them using a hand-operated mangle. Normally, the domestic help did this work, but when extra washing was necessary, these were my duties.

The house had no running water, electricity or gas. A few yards away from the back door was a pump which supplied ground water that had to be boiled before consumption, and heating came from coal and wood fires in the kitchen and dining-room. The lighting downstairs was supplied by paraffin lanterns and ceiling gas lights that used bottled calor gas. Candles lit the rooms upstairs.

Despite these deprivations, in many ways I felt at home. It was very much like my life during childhood and growing up on my parents' farm. Mr Savage was kind towards me, although he was upset when he heard that the courts had delayed their consideration of my case and that Mr Luckett had so far not offered anything in the way of child support. For the time being, Mr Savage agreed to help me financially, and Dot Daniels kept up the supply of second-hand baby clothes.

* * *

The only other human contact I had on the farm, at least until the end of the war, was the farm labourer, an Italian prisoner-of-war who helped Mr Savage, and there were several German prisoners-of-war who worked across the road on the other farm. Their wolf whistles and shouts of "Hallo, fraulein!" annoyed Mr Savage.

We lived off the land. We slaughtered our own animals, usually pigs, we grew our own vegetables and fruit, we milked our own cows and produced butter and cheese, we could catch fish in the nearby pond, or shoot ducks, and my hens were generous with their eggs and meat. The grain from the wheat field was milled into flour that I used for baking bread, and ploughs, horseshoes and other farming equipment were kept in good order by visits to the local blacksmith.

The outlook for child support improved at the start of September 1944 when a Court Order was served on Mr Luckett. The Order required him to pay me a weekly allowance of 15 shillings until my son turned 15, and to reimburse me for the expenses associated with the birth of my child which he still owed. I waited for these payments, but nothing arrived, so my solicitor contacted the court to enforce the Order. I found the wording of the Court Order encouraging except for one phrase which stated that I was responsible for "the delivery of a Bastard Child".

* * *

Late in 1944, my father drove over for a visit and seemed a little more serious than usual. He spent time outside talking to my employer, and when they came in for tea, it was my father who started the conversation.

"Frances Mary, we have an important proposal to make to you. Henry appreciates the assistance you're giving him and knows his health will not improve. He's also aware that you would like to keep your child, and he's willing to support you and permit you to keep your child if you will marry him. Your mother and I like the idea and ask that you agree."

I was at first surprised, then angry and not sure what to say. Here I was, a young woman, still attractive, and still hoping that I might achieve at least some of my early ambitions, but being asked to marry someone more than twice my age, who was very sick and lived miles away from any community. It was a very depressing prospect, and my first reaction was to refuse outright.

On the other hand, after I gave it some thought I realised that, if I said no, I might be thrown out of my parents' home, I might lose my baby, I would find it difficult to secure alternative work, and so far I had no other means of financial support. I had lost my boyfriend, there was not much money left in my bank account, and opportunities for dancing had ceased now that I had a baby to look after, so eventually I had to admit to myself that, for the baby's sake if for no other reason, there did not seem to be any sensible alternative but to agree.

A few weeks later we were wed and I moved in to live with Henry on a permanent basis. He agreed that I should join the local Women's Institute and become a member of the nearest village church. Also, I was asked to enroll in the nursing reserves so that I could better look after him. My mother was delighted with the outcome—so much so that she even agreed to look after John on the day that I was married.

Mr Luckett continued his refusal to pay child support, and according to my solicitor, he claimed that I now had a husband who would look after me, and in any case he could not afford to pay. At the same time, I realised just how isolated my new home was from other human beings.

January 1945 was a whole month of snow and frost when the roads to the farm were blocked by snow drifts, the pond froze over, picking Brussels sprouts was like taking stones off a stalk, and the ground was impenetrable to the spade.

The war in Europe ended on 8th May 1945 following Germany's surrender. We could hear the church bells peel in the nearby village, and there were aircraft circling in formation overhead and disturbing our horses and cattle. On the radio were reports of church services and processions across the country, and for the first time in six years there was also a weather forecast; it predicted a warm and thundery day, with outbreaks of rain. I stayed on the farm, where everything was deathly quiet as usual, but at least I had my son with me, and we quietly celebrated the end of the war together.

CHAPTER 11

GEORGE LUCKETT LOOKED forward to returning home to the Black Country in the centre of England now that the war was over. It had been a very busy time during the past few months, keeping airfields at maximum dispatch, despite congested flying conditions, overseeing the FIDO landing strip near the coast that belonged to Number 4 Bomber Command and, most recently, disposing of equipment and materials that were no longer needed once air and ground crews had returned to civilian life. He was proud of the airfield that he had helped to construct on open fields; it was the biggest project on which he had ever worked, and he thought it was an outstanding success.

The 400 aircrew at the airfield had flown missions most nights from D-Day until 24th April 1945 when the squadron ceased operations. Most sorties were successful, but there were times when aircraft failed to return because their crew members had been killed or taken prisoner. For example, an attack by 300 bombers on an oil plant near the river Rhine on the night of 16th June saw a total of 31 aircraft shot down, including six from his airfield. Active operations included attacks on German gun batteries, troop concentrations, marshalling yards, power stations, oil supply centres, flying-bomb sites, German cities and enemy airfields.

George was angry, however, that during this period, when he was totally immersed in his duties, he had to be distracted by the civil action taken against him by Frances Mary and the York Petty Sessions Court.

An Order was issued that required him to make weekly payments to Frances Mary for the next 15 years, as well as awarding her back payments for expenses she had incurred before and during the birth of her son.

The court adjudged him to be the father of the child and issued an Order that, to his great embarrassment, was delivered by a policeman to his work address on 21st September 1944. He refused to comply, and instead had sent a letter to the court demanding that the amount be varied because he had insufficient funds to fulfill the Order, and he had no idea how much he would earn once the war was over. Nothing further had been heard from the court, but he received information that Frances Mary was now married and had a husband to look after her.

These county-based "petty" courts (since renamed local justice areas) dealt with such matters as minor theft and larceny, assault, drunkenness, bastardy examinations and arbitration. Therefore, the magistrates who supervised these courts had many other matters to attend to already, and the war had brought with it a spike of criminal activity, especially the looting of bombed or damaged buildings, increased juvenile hooliganism because there was nothing better to do, ration book abuse and disregarding wartime rules and regulations, so justice was processed slowly.

Just as George was preparing to go home, he was sent a copy of a letter addressed to Frances Mary's solicitor, requesting that she reappear in front of the court on 24th October 1945 to explain her changed situation and justify her claim. It was appalling that she was harassing him in this way and had not given up on her pursuit of him.

His one anxiety was that the court might write to his home address, or provide Frances Mary with his address so that she could follow up and harass him, and thereby his wife might find out about the child. He decided not to provide his employer with any forwarding details and pretend the event had never happened.

* * *

George was returning to the metropolitan West Midlands to re-engage with his family and resume his career as a civilian civil engineer. He caught a train home, since petrol rationing had restricted private car mileage to 150 miles (240km) a month, about the same distance as it was to his house, although he did purchase a car before he left and garaged it at an airfield. He might have found petrol on the black market, but he knew that, if discovered, he risked losing his driving licence.

His welcome home could not have been more pleasurable. The front door of his house was wide open when he arrived, and his wife Gwen and their two children stood in the doorway. His wife and son ran eagerly down the asphalt driveway to greet him, while his two-year-old daughter was carried by her mother. Everyone breathed a sigh of relief that he was finally home.

Home was by no means extravagant. It was a semi-detached, three-bedroom, two-reception room house built of brick, with the exterior of the upper floor rendered in a white-painted mixture of sand and cement to protect it from damage and dirt. A large, well-maintained garden lay at the rear of the house where his wife grew vegetables. She had prepared a welcome-home meal of potted-meat sandwiches, a mixed salad and an English trifle.

During the meal, he and his wife talked about current events. He asked what had happened to the American soldiers that had been billeted nearby, what had befallen the 'Lancaster' bombers and their pilots, and whether she still had the gas masks and the air-raid shelter in the garden.

"The Americans disappeared before D-Day and we're no longer kept awake by the 'Lancasters' leaving for their nightly visits to Germany," replied Gwen.

"After D-Day, the Americans never returned," she went on, "but several young women from around here have left their families to become war brides. I hope it will work out for them, although some sound more attracted to life in America than to their GI man. Also, it's much quieter now. The nightly gatherings of 'Lancaster' bombers, circling overhead to prepare to fly to Europe, have ended. We didn't use the community air-raid shelters, and the one in our back garden was used only when the sirens sounded; there were very few German bombs dropped in this area. As for the gas masks, they were never needed, and I've stored them away."

George was thrilled to enjoy his best night's sleep for a long time. What mattered to him most was to find a job, and as his parents lived close by, he would get them to help him. His goal was to return to civil engineering that concentrated on residential development and public installations, but finding new employment was not easy. Initially, he joined the architectural department of a city planning office and found himself drafting layouts for prefabricated bungalows, which he found tedious and repetitive. His salary was less than it had been during the war, and he was forced to draw on his meager savings to support his family. He was very certain that he could not afford to pay Frances Mary, even if she won her legal case.

It was fortunate that, during the late 1940s, conditions in civil engineering improved with the introduction of two new Acts of Parliament. Firstly, the Town and Country Planning Act, 1947 established the requirement for planning permission to be obtained from local authorities before any development could begin. Secondly, the Special Roads Act, 1949 sanctioned the construction of a new category of roads known as motorways.

George secured employment in a rapidly growing company that concentrated on residential development, small- to medium-size road construction projects and infrastructure improvements. His working hours were long, and he worked six days a week, but he enjoyed the assignments. He was complimented on the quality of his work, and the pay was good. Partly because he could afford to, and in part because he enjoyed it, he took up drinking more whisky, his pipe smoking continued, and he returned to York to collect his 4-seater Wolseley 14/60 saloon car at the same time as he took up cinephotography.

Nothing was heard from Frances Mary or the magistrates, so he assumed that her efforts to collect child maintenance had failed, and it appeared that she was not pursuing him with any embarrassing correspondence, so he cast off all memories of the people he had known in Yorkshire, including Michael Fromm.

* * *

George felt that the time was right to re-engage with family, and restore the things he used to enjoy as a child. He concentrated on film-making, using the 9.5 mm film format that was popular before the war, and he purchased a camera and projector made by Pathescope. The latter allowed him to project Mickey Mouse cartoons and Laurel and Hardy comedies for his family and friends, and soon he was producing his own films.

George's early pictures were shot near his home because of petrol rationing. The number of miles a person was allowed to travel each month kept changing, but by June 1948 the limit had been set at 90 miles (although it was doubled the following year for the three summer months); to enforce compliance, a red dye was added to petrol that was for commercial use only, and rationing was not ended until May 1950.

Saturday and Sunday outings were normal, and George took his wife with him to watch their two children acting in the films that he directed. There was one production entitled *The Royal Oak* in which his father starred as King Charles, and it was filmed at Boscobel House, famous as the hiding place of King Charles II. Then there was his 1949 production of *Landed Hands*, based on the national campaign "Lend a Hand on the Land" that encouraged urbanites during the years immediately after the war to take their holidays on farms where they could help with farm work.

Once petrol rationing ended, George's film career expanded to other parts of Britain, as there was both petrol and time available for holidays to Weymouth and Portland Bill, with side trips to Lulworth Cove and the Channel Island of Jersey. Jersey became George's favourite place because it was quiet and there were so few people about. He also visited Mousehole in Cornwall and Torquay in Devon.

George and his family celebrated the Queen's Coronation on 2nd June 1953 by attending a sports competition at their local school, followed by a party with cakes and trifle. They watched their son and daughter compete in the sack race, the egg-and-spoon race and the three-legged competition. Memories of the war were rapidly diminishing, although there remained many bombed-out buildings as reminders.

By 1955, the family had upgraded its vehicle to a Jaguar Mark VII saloon, and chose to take a lengthy holiday in Scotland. They travelled from Gretna Green in the south to Dunnet Head in the north, stopping at many places in between.

George greatly appreciated his time off. He could relax and get away from the stress of design, but he began drinking more than he should, and his mood swings started to alarm his wife. There were times when he shouted at her because of something she said or did, and he sometimes lost patience with the children.

However, life in Britain had dramatically improved after the war. New homes were being built as slums were knocked down, rationing was over, and the grief of losing loved ones grew less intense as time did its healing. Life had become generous towards George, and he had no reason to think about Frances Mary.

CHAPTER 12

Michael Fromm chose the wrong time of year to return to Yorkshire, but he did not care about the weather because he was reunited with his girlfriend. At the start of January 1945, it was bitterly cold, with severe frosts and widespread snowfalls, so getting around on his motorbike was dangerous. He returned to the East Riding after several months of supporting bombing missions emanating from United States Air Force bases close to London. Additionally, some aircraft were flying troops and supplies to the battle front, and several squadrons had moved to set up new sites in continental Europe. He gave advice on the design of emergency landing strips, although he was not a participant in the attack on Europe, and he hoped his services would be considered valuable by the American authorities so that he would not face problems when he returned to California.

He enjoyed reconnecting with the people he had known when he left the airfield just before D-Day, although George Luckett was not one of them. Apparently, George remained living on an air base some distance from where Michael lodged and had not been seen recently.

Weather-wise, it was an unpleasant few days. There were several nights when bombing raids were cancelled because the airfield was snowbound, and when attacks resumed, pilots had to deal with severe snow squalls and awful visibility. Ground crews worked long hours trying to keep the runways clear.

Michael worried that his girlfriend Alice might find someone else because British troops were soon to begin returning home. Consequently, he arrived at her home with pairs of stockings and a powder compact for Alice, cigarettes for her father and bars of chocolate for her mother. Alice was delighted and told him not to worry about the relationship; she said she was in love with him and would marry him as soon as she reached the age of 21. Her parents had come to terms with the alliance, but they were still shaken when they heard that she would live with Michael in America once they were married. She was their only daughter, so they did not want to lose her to a foreign land.

While he was visiting the south-east of England, Michael had hoped to go to London to enjoy its attractions. However, a week after D-Day, on 13th June 1944, the first V-1 or "doodlebug", a bomb with wings but no pilot, descended on London, and some 2,500 of these bombs were launched on England during the following two weeks. Tremendous damage was caused, even though many of the missiles were shot down by anti-aircraft fire over the Channel or by fighter 'planes before they arrived at their destination. Apparently, the bombs were launched from mobile vehicles that were based in France and moved around by the Germans so that they would stay hidden from enemy aircraft. Michael decided to stay away.

* * *

Another year needed to elapse before he could marry Alice, so he had to find a job now that he was back in Yorkshire. He would have to compete with returning military personnel for factory work, office employment and regular labouring, so he chose to look for something else that would use his specific skills. As well as his engineering qualifictions, he was proficient in German and considered himself to be especially well qualified for work in one of the growing number of prisoner-of-war camps where captured Germans were incarcerated. The Yorkshire War Agricultural Executive Committee was the county establishment responsible for organising prisoners to work on farms, so he contacted this organisation and was offered work at a prison camp situated only 15 miles (25km) from where his girlfriend lived.

The role of the Executive Committee was to safeguard the nation's food supplies by negotiating crop selection and quotas with farmers and helping them to obtain the resources required to achieve these targets, in addition to assigning work to prisoners. Michael believed he knew a little about farming, and he could converse with both the farmers and the prisoners, and he therefore thought he would be an ideal employee. The number of German prisoners-of-war in Britain was rising dramatically, and by 1946 it had reached around 400,000. Several hundred towns hosted prison camps, and around 20 percent of all farm workers were prisoners-of-war.

Earlier in the war, the camps had also housed Italian prisoners, but following Italy's surrender in September 1943, they were transferred to low-security camps and replaced with so-called 'military guests' from Germany. Most prisoners were shipped to either Britain or the United States, and in Britain they were processed through interrogation centres and then transferred by rail to their designated internment camp. The prison to which they were sent partly depended on the prison code they were given after interrogation. Non-Nazis were graded white, those with uncertain loyalties were coded grey and those with strong party affiliations were classified as black. The darker the grading, the further away from London the prisoner was sent, and the more remote the camp. The camp that employed Michael had about 1,200 prisoners who were mainly considered low-risk.

Close to his new place of work, Michael found accommodation in an old manor house on the edge of a meadow sloping down to the banks of a slow-moving river. Its situation was a few minutes away from the centre of the nearby market town, and Michael frequently rode his motorbike to the central square to buy fish and chips. He always ordered "one of each with scraps" (cod and chips with deep-fried batter pieces left over in the fryer), which he could smell frying in the shop long before he saw the square.

For nearly twelve months, Michael was one of the prison administrators. His task was to assign inmates to farms based on farmers' needs, and to arrange for prisoners to be transported, preferably by lorry, each day. His prisoners had a reputation for hard work and were usually scheduled to work six days a week from 9am to 5pm. Until Germany surrendered, guards normally accompanied the prisoners to their assignments, although some of the better-behaved ones were allowed to billet overnight on their assigned farms. Romances flourished between prisoners, the daughters of their hosts and Land Girls, as they all worked together in the fields.

Social activities were offered, including a programme of re-education to explain the evils of the Nazi regime. Prisoners could learn English, attend music events, play soccer and write letters home, as long as they were read and censored before posting. Their treatment was strict but humane, and public reaction to prisoners stemmed more from curiosity and indifference than fear. To those captured soldiers with a sense of humour, arrival in the camp was the fulfillment of Hitler's promise at the start of the war that they would soon be in England! Confidence grew daily that the war would end soon.

Prisoner repatriation began after VE-Day, although the last ones to leave Michael's camp did not depart until 1949. Michael ended his employment during January 1946 and prepared to return to California. His plan was to marry Alice, enjoy a brief honeymoon in Scarborough, then travel to San Francisco via London and, once home, arrange for his wife's non-quota immigration so that she could follow him without a visa.

* * *

Michael and Alice were married in a small church, and those present were only Alice's immediate family and a close friend. Alice looked lovely, despite the limited availability of make-up and the beetroot juice she used as lipstick. She stood there in her bright red dress, with its tiny brass buttons and activity skirt, showing off her soft black hair, her porcelain complexion slightly damaged by the sun and work on the farm, and her innocent pale-green eyes. New clothes were rationed, and a 'Make Do and Mend' campaign had been introduced in 1942 to encourage sewing, knitting and the recycling of old clothes to make new ones at knitting parties arranged by the local Women's Institute.

In place of a wedding reception, just a light tea was served in the farmhouse before the couple left for their two-night honeymoon in Scarborough. The family wedding gift was a tea pot with matching cups and saucers. Alice's parents were happy for their daughter, but they remained upset that she would soon leave for America. It was such a long way to California and, as farmers, they could not leave their farm for any length of time. They were also concerned about money, as travel was very expensive, and Alice shared their concerns.

Once the honeymoon was over, the couple separated so that Michael could travel home to the United States, both to try to find a flat to rent in San Francisco and also to finalise arrangements for his wife to join him there. He knew that, as he had been away for several years, his parents would be pleased that he was returning home, and they would be excited to meet their new daughter-in-law.

Immigration papers had to be approved before Alice could follow Michael to the United States, although fortunately in December 1945 the US War Bride Act had been passed, and it exempted the foreign-born wives and children of US military personnel from immigration quotas. Michael believed Alice would qualify for the exemption because of his work which he thought classified him as a civilian employee of the US military. He was not alone in finding a British wife, as approximately 70,000 GI war brides left Britain after the war.

Michael's departure from Yorkshire was by train, once he had sold his trusted BSA motorbike. The railways were the main means of transport during the war, and they were still serving a vital role for prisoners who were beginning to be repatriated, and military personnel who were on their way home. Some hours later, he was in Kings Cross station in London, having had to stand most of the way because the carriages were packed with Army, Navy and Air Force personnel.

His stay in London was brief. Bomb damage was widespread, with large tracts of housing destroyed, buildings badly damaged and rubble everywhere. Even Buckingham Palace had not escaped the German bombs, and in fact the palace was specifically targeted and attacked on several occasions, causing damage to the buildings as well as to the gardens. Sightseeing and moving around the city was out of the question, but it was nonetheless pleasurable not to have to worry about the threat of German bombing, and to wave goodbye to the blackout that had ended during April 1945.

Michael wanted to return home quickly. He had thought at first about hitching a ride on one of the Liberty boats, but he decided to return as speedily as he could. London's Heathrow Airport was not yet open for civilian passengers, but a limited air service existed between Croydon and New York. The ticket was expensive, but he could afford the fare, and fifteen hours after leaving London he was home in the United States, thanks to an American Overseas Airline's DC-4 that made a few stops on the way in Shannon, Northern Ireland, in Gander, Newfoundland, and in Boston.

Three days later, Michael was back home with his parents in Sacramento, having crossed the United States by train. They were grateful to have him home, as well as knowing that their Belgian relatives were safe after the end of the Battle of the Bulge in the Ardennes a year earlier.

Inside their home everything looked familiar, but outside the landscape had dramatically changed, and the City of Trees was becoming a city of people. Gone were the open spaces and tight neighborhoods, as surges of people were arriving after the war had ended in Asia six months earlier, so box-like houses were being created on the city outskirts. The spacious orchards and fields of Michael's youth were beginning to disappear under concrete foundations and wooden shingles, and businesses were popping up everywhere to make use of the new labour supply. Michael decided to move to San Francisco, bought a car and rented a flat on 6th and Lawton.

* * *

Some weeks later, he received permission to bring his wife to America. It was a time of mixed emotions for Alice, as she was excited at the thought of a new life with her new husband in America, but sorrowful at having to bid farewell to her family and friends as she began to pack and prepare for the long and arduous journey to San Francisco. She joined several hundred other women, some with babies, on an American steamer headed to New York. She spent 16 days at sea, much of the time talking with other women, sitting on crowded decks and gazing out to sea at grey skies and choppy waves. Some people became sick, but she did not, and after she arrived in New York she had an arduous three-day train journey on a "war bride" service to California.

It was a scary start because everything so was unfamiliar, from the way that Americans drove on the wrong side of the road, to the use of a strange currency and the unusual accents she kept hearing. Nonetheless, she made it to the West Coast where she received a huge kiss from Michael as she dismounted from the train at the station. He immediately introduced her to his parents, who were delighted to meet their daughter-in-law for the first time. Alice did not know if she would fit in, but Michael's parents were kind and thoughtful, and they promised to introduce her to their friends, show her around San Francisco and patiently explain anything that Alice did not understand.

CHAPTER 13

The highlight of Alice's first week in San Francisco was the discovery of the huge food stores. She had never seen anything quite like them. There were so many groceries from which to choose, and she could buy anything she liked, with varieties of fruit, vegetables and cuts of meat that she had never seen before. Nor was there any rationing, except for sugar. She found bananas and ate them for the first time in many years. Michael was delighted as he watched his wife gleefully inspect and select items that sometimes were totally new to her. Cigarettes were cheaper than those back home in England, so she began to smoke.

There were also chemist shops, or drug stores as Michael called them, selling everything from pills and medicine to cosmetics and toiletries. Travelling to the stores was very convenient here; in Yorkshire, other than by walking, only the car, bicycle or an occasional bus were available, but in San Francisco there were lots of buses, cable cars and street cars. She also had a refrigerator in the kitchen of the apartment Michael had found, as well as several other electric appliances that Michael showed her how to use. The rooms were much larger, the furniture chunkier and more comfortable, and the motorcars were huge.

It was a wonderful first few weeks as Michael took her to places that he had visited as a boy growing up. They made journeys to the Delta, the Gold Country, Lake Tahoe and the Santa Cruz redwoods and beaches. Also, his love of music and dancing had not gone away.

He loved flipping gramophone records to listen to Frank Sinatra, Perry Como and big band music, and he took Alice to several jazz concerts.

They attended jitterbug dances, and Alice mastered the steps to the Lindy Hop, Collegiate Shag and West Coast Swing. These dances were very different from the foxtrot, quickstep and waltz that she was used to back home. She had rarely been allowed into pubs during her adolescent years, because they were not considered to be suitable places for a woman, and certainly not for one who was unaccompanied. She therefore found it exciting when Michael introduced her to bars, where she often drank cocktails or spirits, instead of the usual soft drinks and the occasional glass of sherry that she would have had back home. Now she knew why so many men frequented pubs: Beer was not rationed during the war, so Michael told her!

They also went to the "movies", not the "pictures", and Alice enjoyed eating hamburgers, hot dogs and fried chicken in place of fish and chips, Yorkshire pudding and British 'bangers' (sausages).

She wrote to tell her mother about her experiences, and she received an update from her parents on what was happening at home. The farm situation had improved because the government had introduced financial incentives for farmers to convert unused land to pasture, and at the same time to expand the acreage of arable land. Rationing unfortunately continued for petrol and food items, causing the black market to prosper for groceries such as flour, butter and eggs. Most women had to go back to living a life of domesticity as, encouraged by the government, many firms barred the employment of married women.

The airfield remained open, although it had been downsized to focus on training and transportation, and none of the people Michael knew were still there. Additionally, the airfield had taken on the role of being one of the arrival points for VIPs visiting York.

* * *

The evenings in San Francisco were filled with romantic love and tender touches as the couple spent most of their time together, but it was soon evident to Michael that financially he needed work. Alice volunteered to get a job, but Michael said "no".

There were multiple opportunities for Michael because California was developing its infrastructure in response to a rapidly growing population. Residential tract development was underway, and extensions were being built to runways and terminals at major airports. Probably the biggest and most complex projects involved the development of the state's highway system, so this is where Michael found work, accepting regular invitations to visit the State Department of Public Works in Sacramento, and also calling in on his parents at the same time. His duties involved site assessments, pavement design and feasibility studies. Soon he and Alice had sufficient funds to buy a home in the Sunset district, just before Alice became pregnant, and in the summer of 1949 she gave birth to a daughter they called Emma. Alice's mother insisted on flying out to see her granddaughter, and that turned out to be the only time she made the long trip to America.

As the 1950s arrived, Alice was at home taking care of her daughter, and Michael continued his commitment to building freeways, supporting construction of a new network of roads in the Los Angeles region. However, in 1952 when Emma was only three, she was found playing with two boys who lived next door with their grandparents. Their father, a keen fisherman, had been fishing for steelhead on the Klamath River during a summer weekend when he mistakenly used a cup that belonged to a person with a mild form of poliomyelitis. Unfortunately, the virus can be transferred by oral and nasal contact, so he became infected. He eventually recovered much of the use of his body, but he remained paralysed down his left side. His wife and eldest son also contracted milder forms of the disease, but once he had been diagnosed, his two younger boys were sent to live with their grandparents in the hope that they would not be infected. Alice and Michael were very worried that Emma might have contracted the illness from the boys, as it was a highly infectious disease that could cause death by asphyxiation. Fortunately, Emma stayed well.

The other event that caused the family great concern was the outbreak of the Korean War during June 1950. At first it seemed a long way away, despite local exhibits of air-raid shelters (although they had more to do with the Cold War), but when missile installations were built in reaction to the risk of air attacks, including aircraft carrying nuclear weapons, the situation became much more serious.

Alice wrote to her mother to tell her about what was happening, only to hear back that the Americans had taken over the local airfield because of the Korean War, and they were stationing missiles nearby. There had been an outcry from the local community, which was concerned that these medium-range ballistic missiles would attract attacks from other countries, thereby risking the safety of the local people. The missiles stayed where they were, however, despite the protests.

Finally, just as Emma began school in 1954, the US Supreme Court ruled that racial segregation in public education was illegal. Clearly, the nature of Emma's education was about to change, although Alice thought it a change for the better, as there was nothing similar in Britain. By now Alice felt she was a true American and loved her adopted country, appreciated its freedoms, respected its flag and enjoyed its diversity.

Thus, as 1956 arrived, there was peace and happiness in the Fromm household, and Michael was planning to celebrate their tenth wedding anniversary with a two-week holiday in Hawaii accompanied by his parents.

CHAPTER 14

I FELT LONELY AND isolated on a farm that was located in the middle of a moor, even though there was an atmosphere of celebration elsewhere in Britain once the war ended in Europe on 8th May 1945 and in Asia on 14th August 1945. A two-day national holiday was declared after Japan surrendered, but this did not extend to the farm where my daily routine was uninterrupted. Instead, during the next several years, I found myself confronted with a series of new challenges that were as daunting as they were unforeseen.

In the first place, the Italian prisoner-of-war who had helped out on the farm since 1941 was repatriated. This meant that Henry had to take over all the farm work himself, which was much more than he had ever done before. The extra, heavy workload affected his daily dosage of insulin, resulting in him regularly taking the wrong amount. I would find him collapsed outside in the fields or among the farm buildings, and when he came inside, he would sometimes become violent. I did my best to look after him, but there were times when our quarrels turned physical. I blamed these incidents on his medical condition and would call the doctor if the situation grew too threatening.

Secondly, he became increasingly angry with me because I was not receiving any child support. He had stopped paying my wages when we married, and he now believed that it was my responsibility to pay for the upkeep of my son. I had to rely on my father for funds and Dot Daniels for baby clothes.

During October 1945, I was required to appear in court to request that the child support Order be enforced, but whatever the magistrates thought or did, their actions had no effect on Mr Luckett. Nothing was received, and Henry became angrier. I thought about writing to Mr Luckett, but I did not know his full address, and the solicitor cautioned that I should not interfere with matters that were the responsibility of the court.

What we grew on the farm also became an issue. Henry, as a farmer, was expected to fulfill the government's agricultural policy that at the time involved maximising food production by converting pasture land into arable use. Because of his health, this was not practical and we had to remain farming only livestock and hens. This affected our income, and the only other modest addition to our earnings was from someone who worked in the local sugar beet factory, who bicycled to the farm and traded sugar for eggs. This inability to change the purpose of the farm aggravated Henry's attitude towards my son.

Once John reached the age of 2, my older sister would collect him and have him spend several weeks at a time with her and husband in order to keep him out of the way of Henry's anger and give him a bit of a break from the strictness of his upbringing. Sadly, this arrangement ended when their first child was born and John was only six.

In the meantime, I had become friendly with the people on the farm across the road, so John would then spend large parts of his days with their son whom he called "Big John". In this way, he was protected from the worst arguments I had with Henry, but the situation became more complex when I gave birth to a daughter and my life became more restricted. Any freedom I had hoped to enjoy when I was married seemed to have disappeared.

This distressful situation worsened during the winter of 1947 when a vicious cold spell hit our home from late January to mid-March, with drifting snow and severe frosts devastating the farm. The roads were blocked, we had no coal deliveries, on most days the milk could not be collected, sheep and lambs died of hypothermia in the fields, potatoes and apples rotted in storage and root vegetables were frozen in the ground. Pigs stayed warm inside their pigsties with heat lamps, and hens huddled in their coops, with sacking that blocked out the draughts.

I suppose conditions could have been worse if we had had the advantage of distributed utilities in our home. As it was, the water pipes did not freeze because we did not have any, and the outside water pump continued to work as long as we poured hot water on it before it was operated. Power outages were frequent across the country, but we had no electricity service. One positive development from the cold spell was the government's decision to nationalise electric power and create a national transmission grid. Very quickly, electricity pylons appeared across our fields and around us, and we soon had electricity in the home that allowed us to enjoy improved lighting, electric fires, hot water and an electric cooker.

I also had responsibility for changing my son's name. He still carried my maiden name, so the idea was to shield him from embarrassment at school by changing his surname to that of Henry's family. My solicitor helped me with these arrangements, and he told me that the name change would not affect the Court Order, so I proceeded. Therefore, during August 1947 my son's surname was changed by Deed Poll to Savage. The only person disappointed by the alteration was my father who, with only daughters in his family, had hoped that John would continue to carry his surname.

Henry reluctantly continued to provide food for my son and a roof over his head, although he remained very angry with me. I was pregnant again, which seemed to reduce his hostility, and in spring 1948 I bore him a son. John then had the companionship of a sister and a brother.

Unfortunately, John's name change did not protect him from all forms of bullying, as I discovered during one of my visits to see my parents. He wandered away from their house into the village and returned an hour later with his face covered in cow manure. I asked him what happened, and he told me that a girl a few doors away had shouted at him from the rungs of her farm gate that she was not allowed to talk to him. She had told him to go away and then picked up some soft cow dung and thrown it at him. I cleaned him up and nothing more was said of the incident.

Now that I had three children, and my mother had at last forgiven me for the past, we developed a tradition of spending Christmas with my family. Henry would drive us to my parents' home on Christmas Day morning, then return to the farm and tend the livestock, and collect us three or four days later. Christmas dinner was with my parents, Boxing Day was at my older sister's home, and a day or so later we would drive over to my younger sister's home for tea. She had married and lived a few minutes away from my parents.

In September 1949, John began school; each morning he was collected by school bus and driven five miles to his classroom. In the evening, the bus dropped him off a quarter of a mile away, and he walked home. The barking of our sheepdog was the signal that he was about to arrive. Until then he had lived a life in almost total seclusion on our remote farm, but once at school he was exposed to a whole range of illnesses, and he suffered in turn from measles, chicken pox, whooping cough and mumps. This meant that I had to work even harder to look after him, although my home help continued her daily work and assisted me.

Otherwise, school seemed to go well for John, and because he spent a lot of time outdoors, I soon began to help him with his hobby of collecting birds' eggs. I guided him on how to identify his eggs and prepare them for storage, and which bird species to trade at school. He also participated in the school's rose hip picking campaign during autumn. The rose hips were used in the manufacture of rose hip syrup, an important source of vitamin C, which was in short supply after the war, and he received three pence for every pound he collected. This also took him outdoors and away from his stepfather.

I gave him an allotment in the garden to grow lettuces that he took and sold in the local marketplace alongside me when I went to sell eggs. He charged two pence for each head, so we both made a little bit of money.

By the early 1950s, my husband had taken a lasting dislike towards John, who now spent much of his time with our neighbours across the road. To gain some freedom, I decided to become the President of the local village's Women's Institute and attend nursing classes, as this would also mean that I could better help Henry with his illness. Whenever needed, my mother came to babysit the children.

Unfortunately, my husband's health continued to worsen, and during 1952 the doctor admitted him to hospital, where he stayed for 27 weeks. It was a difficult period for me, with three young children to look after, as well as taking care of the sheep and hens, which were my duties while he was gone. A close farmer friend came each day to milk the cows by hand and feed the pigs and ferrets, as I always hated the ferrets that Henry used for rat catching.

By the time Henry was discharged from hospital, the government had issued instructions that farmers should plough out their grassland and convert it to cereal growing, but Henry's health did not allow him to do this. Thus, with great reluctance, we sold the farm and moved to a small-holding (a house with an adjacent plot of land smaller than a farm) during April 1953. Located in the nearest village, it was a comfortable house with running water, electricity and even a telephone. It became even more luxurious when we installed an indoor toilet and bathroom and purchased our first television.

We also started the annual tradition of taking a week's holiday by the sea, in addition to sending our children on Sunday school outings to Scarborough and Whitby. My own first holiday was during 1948 when Henry drove me to Blackpool. Travel was something I had always wanted to do, but by the time I was old enough, war had broken out.

My son progressed well at primary school, then passed the examinations that allowed him to go on to grammar school, and I was very proud of his accomplishment. Very early each day he left home by school bus, and was taken to York, and then he was delivered home in the same manner during early evening. Having left school myself at 15, I was unable to give him much academic help, and unfortunately, at the end of his first year in July 1956, I received a bundle of school reports that caused me great disappointment. For different subjects, he had been evaluated by his teachers as "mediocre", "a rather a low standard" and "he has very little aptitude for this subject". What dismayed me most was the evaluation from the headmaster: "Most disappointing, and there must be a great improvement next term or we shall have to ask ourselves if he is fit for the sort of teaching we do here."

I thought the evaluations were more a reflection of his upbringing than his intellectual abilities, and I found the assessments totally unacceptable. I had not sacrificed the past twelve years to produce a "mediocre" son, so I talked to a retired headmistress living in the village about what should be done. Her advice was to visit the school and discuss the situation with John's teachers. As far as my husband was concerned, John's assessments did not matter because he wanted my son out of school and earning a wage the moment he turned 15. What lay ahead of me was yet another daunting challenge.

CHAPTER 15

As 1956 arrived, George Luckett continued his successful career, but at home he became more irritable and impatient, and he expected instant obedience and cooperation from his family when he gave them instructions. Most of the time he was cheerful, but he could be unpredictable and menacing, and everyone assumed that his behavior was caused by his stress and long hours of work. One of his projects was designing a prestigious new home for his family, and several times he alleged that they did not appreciate his generosity. His wife chose to disregard his tantrums, but they did not go away.

He no longer thought about Frances Mary and was pleased with himself that his wife was unaware of what had happened in Yorkshire. After all, Frances Mary was now married, so he assumed that the responsibility for her illegitimate son had shifted to her husband.

During late 1955, he developed an irritating, persistent cough and sore throat, and he blamed his illness on the cold and foggy weather. Gwen, however, raised the alarm when he started losing weight, coughing up small amounts of blood and was kept awake by nighttime sweating. She called their doctor, who examined George and arranged for a series of X-rays to be taken, with shocking results. George had contracted the bacterial infection of tuberculosis, a potentially fatal lung disease spread in the air and transmitted by others through coughs and sneezes. He had no idea where it came from.

No one was certain which stage of the illness George had reached. They did not know if he were only infected, meaning that the bacteria were inactive, or if it were actively spreading through his body. If the latter, he would be highly contagious. The doctor's diagnosis was that it had reached the active stage, so he advised George to move to a separate room in the house as a precaution against passing the infection on to his family. He should rest and eat good food, but if he showed no signs of improvement, he would have to be moved to a sanatorium for residential treatment.

George's food containers, cutlery, glassware, towels, bed linen, toiletries and other personal items were marked with his name and kept in his room for his use only. Anyone going to see him had to wear a face mask, and the door to his room was kept closed at all times, although his windows were left open to allow in fresh air, even if it were sometimes foggy outside. His children were allowed to visit him, but instructed to stay away from his bedside, and his parents were frequent visitors.

The hope was that the illness would be cured by this treatment, but that did not happen. The doctor gave each family member a skin test to determine whether they were also infected. When no bumps appeared around the area of the injection, he told them they were disease-free but should stay away from George as much as possible.

It was a stressful time for Gwen. She heard that George's recovery might take as long as 12 to 18 months, and she was told that she needed to find a suitable sanitarium for him. The danger was that, if he did not receive treatment, he could develop a more serious strain of tuberculosis that could cause death. However, this is not what George wanted; he wanted no treatment at all, just to get back to work. Eventually Gwen found on the Norfolk coast, about 200 miles (320km) away, a private, very expensive, open-air sanatorium with a first-class reputation for excellence in treating pulmonary tuberculosis. The hospital was not busy, and each patient was given a private, south-facing room with access to the lawn outside. Because of modern progress in the treatment of tuberculosis, there were few patients so George was welcome and would be well-treated. His parents assisted with the fees.

George's response to his illness at home was erratic. At first he accepted the condition, but then isolation turned him argumentative and aggressive, and he objected to not being allowed outside. He became sullen and depressed, asked to smoke, and when that was denied, requested whisky.

It was with much sadness and worry about the future that Gwen packed his suitcase, sat him upright on the back seat of the car, supported by pillows, and left for the sanatorium. The children stayed behind in the care of George's parents, wondering if they would ever see their father alive again.

Gwen was conscious that she was now in charge of the family and apprehensive of what might happen. It would not be easy to cope on her own with both children in their teens, and her son about to leave school and needing help finding a career. The family no longer received any income, as her husband had lost his job, although George's parents said they would give their support.

For his part, George was annoyed that he was being sent away, and upset that his employment had been terminated. Eventually, he gave up wondering about how he had contracted the disease and accepted that he had no alternative but to move into the sanatorium. He decided that he would cure himself quickly and then find a new job. He had no intention of dying.

* * *

Gwen enjoyed the drive and was impressed by the beautiful location of the sanatorium at the end of a long, narrow lane about a mile (1.6km) from the sea. The treatment offered there was fashioned after the German and Swiss hospitals that had pioneered the method of focussing the patient on eating good food and doing nothing in the fresh air. There was no actual medical treatment; each resident was supposed to sit and relax all day, giving their body and mind total rest, and were not supposed to move except to visit the toilet. They sat on the lawn in deck chairs, and were propped up by pillows; they were encouraged to read, but told to avoid all physical activity. Near the end of their stay there was an opportunity for some convalescence during which they could engage in light pursuits such as playing with dice, putting at golf, playing pool or taking pottery-making lessons.

The facilities for healing included a number of movable wooden cabins out on the lawn; these were "airing huts" that the patients could individually occupy in the case of poor weather. The cabins were scattered across the tree-studded gardens, and close to each was a small wooden construction that served as a toilet.

George hated the setting. He was quarantined with only fellow patients to talk to, he had nothing much to do, and any special requests usually went disregarded by the nurses. He was thoroughly bored, yet told to rest if he wanted to recover quickly. He tried to read, but he found that monotonous, so he would stop after a while and fall asleep. When he was allowed to, he enjoyed the company of other patients, and he appreciated his wife's visits at least once a month, and more frequently if authorised by the sanatorium.

During her visits, Gwen gave him updates of what was happening at home, and she volunteered to find a job when she was running out of money, but George did not want her to work and always countered her suggestion with a promise to write to his parents. He often complained about the slowness of his recovery, and claimed that he was already recovered and should be taken home.

A more or less standard daily routine was in place by the time George reached his first anniversary at the sanatorium, and it was during March 1957 that Gwen arrived one day, appearing upset and worried. George reacted to her mood and quickly asked, "Is anything wrong? You seem preoccupied."

"I'm very upset," Gwen reluctantly replied, trying hard to restrain her anger. "I've received this nasty document that you need to see, and I want to know what you were up to while you were in Yorkshire."

With that, she took out of her purse an official-looking, small manila envelope and handed the document to George. He saw that it came from the Clerk to the Justices for a Petty Sessional Court in Yorkshire, and it was addressed to his home. It requested immediate remittance of back-payments for child support and an explanation for the cause of the delay in payment. It also reminded him that he was responsible for maintenance of the child until it reached the age of 15. He had spent years thinking that this was all behind him, so he was devastated that his secret was out and he hesitated about what to say.

"But this was a long time ago," he claimed, adding, "Where did it come from?"

"It arrived a few days ago when two policemen came to the house," Gwen explained. "They were looking for you, and I told them you were here, but they refused to leave until I accepted this letter. They didn't tell me what it was about, so I opened it."

George remained silent, looked away from Gwen and tapped nervously on the letter. He did not reply immediately, as he was not sure whether to deny or admit what was implied by the letter, although he realised that denial would risk Gwen's disbelief.

"That all happened many years ago," George began. "I didn't think it was important to tell you in the middle of a war, and I didn't want to upset you. I never went out with this woman and I'm still not sure that I'm the father. She married someone else and I thought that was the end of the story. I'm so sorry that you had to find out this way."

"And so you should be," Gwen lashed out. "How could you be so dishonest? How could you be so unfaithful? How can I trust you in the future? Was it just this one time, or did it happen again?"

George was overcome with guilt, although he was irritated by his wife's accusation, and he still was unsure how to answer, as he hoped to get some sympathy from his wife in view of the condition of his health.

"Look," he said, trying to placate her, "it wasn't my fault that the courts believed the woman rather than me, and I don't think I should have to pay now she's married. There's been no-one else, and I'm truly sorry that you had to find out this way. It happened such a long time ago that I'd forgotten all about it."

"But it happened!" Gwen asserted.

"Yes," replied George, "but I never went out with this woman. It all happened so quickly while I was lodging with her family. Since then, I've always been faithful to you and the children."

"Just know that I'm disgusted with you and it won't be easy to forgive you," Gwen was still furious. "For the time being, I'll worry about your illness and not the letter, but we'll see how I feel when you're back home. I have no intention of telling the children."

With that, the conversation ended, and Gwen excused herself, although she was not sure what to do. On the one hand, she could no longer trust her husband, and his deceit appalled her, but she now had two children to think about, her husband had nearly died of tuberculosis, the event had happened a long time ago, and she thought her husband was repentant. George had told her that he would take care of answering the letter and she should not worry.

He repeatedly read the letter after Gwen had left, and became increasingly annoyed that he was being harassed by the court. He sat down and penned a reply to the effect that he would consider paying the arrears, but not for the periods when he was out of work, and he would begin remittances only when he either had a job or was receiving unemployment benefits. The letter was sent, and he heard nothing further from the Magistrate's Clerk.

Gwen maintained her regular visits, but the discovery of his parenting a child in Yorkshire had chilled the relationship. She kept her promise not to tell anyone, but she no longer had any faith in him.

* * *

By June 1957, George had returned home, but Gwen found it impossible to forgive him. He had been dishonest, and while she had no reason to believe anything similar happened after he left Yorkshire, she felt that she could no longer rely on him to tell the truth. Meanwhile, their son had left school, and the plan was for him to work with his father once George found a job. Their 14-year-old daughter was still at school, and she was interested in studying occupational therapy, having watched her mother deal with her father's illness.

George now looked much older, and he was warned by the sanatorium to be careful and not work too hard. He was told that he should take regular tests to be sure he stayed clear of the infection.

Once home, his first objective was to find work. His previous employers had no interest in him, but there were many other opportunities as post-war development continued to boom. Flats and low-rise apartments were sprouting up everywhere to replace slums, while there were road works all over the place and other infrastructure projects were widespread.

Initially, he received a job offer from a local authority. However, it involved him in accepting a level of responsibility that was no higher than the rank he had reached during the 1930s. The eventual solution came from his parents. They proposed that he form his own construction company, hire his son and they would finance the business. Gwen was offered the position of company secretary, which she accepted on the understanding that she could do most of the work from home. At last George was once again energised, enthusiastic and confident that he would return to his profession and continue his success. He also started to construct his new family home.

His business became a very successful enterprise during the late 1950s. He concentrated on projects that involved building public-owned housing, known as council houses, and also struck deals with local authorities that involved road-widening, bridge-strengthening and bus station expansion. Another opportunity came from replacing traffic lights with roundabouts, to speed up traffic flow.

His success was not to last forever, however. By early 1960, construction contracts were becoming much larger and more complex than his small firm could cope with. There were motorways to be built, rather than road widening, and high-rise "tower" blocks for housing instead of council houses. He soon began to find that projects were difficult to come by without creating additional financing, and sometimes he was forced to partner a general contractor for a specific part of a project.

These changes agitated him, and he brought home his anger and frustration to take out on his family. He would rant and rave, disagreeing over trifles, and never seemed able to settle down and relax at home. The firm's financial condition worsened when most of his expensive construction equipment was stolen, but nothing was ever his fault. He would blame his son and his wife for making mistakes, and launch tirades against his competitors for his lack of business. Predictions were made that his firm was going out of business, and his suppliers increasingly complained about the delayed payment of invoices. Gwen was increasingly alarmed when George started to come home late in the evening after drinking bouts in a pub, when he would physically abuse her and the children. It seemed to worsen as time went by, so she eventually called their doctor again.

* * *

This time there was yet another upsetting diagnosis. George was evaluated as having a mental disorder that impaired his social functioning and that, if not addressed, might lead to suicide. At first he was prescribed with newly-discovered antipsychotic medications, but unfortunately these brought about a series of side effects including anxiety, nervousness, agitation and headaches. Therefore, his health did not respond, and Gwen worried that he might do harm to her and children, never mind to himself.

The doctor suggested that George needed psychiatric help and recommended that he undergo therapy as an inpatient at a local mental health asylum. George was appalled by the idea that he be placed in what he termed "a loony bin", and secured the support of his parents in rejecting the suggestion. For several weeks he stubbornly refused to accede to the doctor's proposal, and he became ever more violent and abusive at home, and also irrational at work. Gwen decided that there was no way the family could stay together under these circumstances, so she persuaded the doctor to arrange for the compulsory detention of her husband in a mental hospital where he would receive treatment against his will. Sectioning, as this process was called, certified that he was suffering from a severe mental disorder, required medical treatment and must be forcibly placed under psychiatric care. Gwen was relieved, but George was livid, and his parents refused to talk to her after this decision was taken.

Like the sanitarium, the hospital was well-equipped and had a first-rate reputation for successful medication and psychiatric help. There were approximately 1,200 psychiatric beds in the institution, and the mental treatment given to George included electroconvulsive therapy.

Under the Mental Health Act, 1959, doctors possessed the authority to treat George without his approval and keep him in hospital for as long as they chose, and for at least several weeks. He received regular treatments which involved having electrodes attached to both sides of his head through which he received a series of electrical stimulations. This therapy was given to him every other day, and he hated it. He tried to resist all treatment and discharge himself, but he was detained inside involuntarily for approximately six weeks before being released early in 1961. He was "deinstitutionalised" after signs of improvement, and went home for continuing care and treatment. Everyone was afraid of him and of what might happen if he lost his temper.

Meanwhile, the family had moved into its new home designed and built by George a few miles from where they had lived formerly. This had no effect on George; his behavior did not improve, his business headed deeper into bankruptcy, he continued to drink too much, and his wife moved into a separate bedroom. His son continued to work for him under difficult circumstances, but his daughter moved away from home to study for an Occupational Therapy qualification in Exeter in the south of England.

* * *

Approximately two years later, in early 1963, George simply disappeared. It had been a strained relationship for some months, and Gwen and George no longer talked much to each other except to argue. On this particular morning, his wife went downstairs to find his car missing, and it appeared that he had taken with him some of his belongings. She was surprised because he did not normally leave so early, and she wondered if he had left on a business trip.

That evening, there was a knock on the door. When Gwen answered it, she found two official-looking, tall-helmeted police constables standing on her pathway and looking very anxious about the purpose of their visit, and her first reaction was to imagine that something bad had happened to one of her children. The constables first greeted her and then sought to establish that they were talking to the wife of Mr George Luckett.

"We have some difficult news for you, Mrs Luckett," the more senior of the two policemen spoke compassionately but directly.

"What has happened?" Gwen asked, terrified that one of her children might have been harmed or done something wrong.

"It's your husband," the constable replied. "We need to notify you of his death. It appears that he must have killed himself today, because we found his car abandoned next to the Clifton Suspension Bridge, near Bristol, and we believe that he must have jumped from the railings of the bridge. The car we found is a dark green Jaguar that is registered in your husband's name, and there was nothing inside the vehicle except a suitcase. We've spent the day searching the river, but so far we have not found anything. It's been raining, so it's possible that his body could have been washed away by the high tide, but we'll continue looking tomorrow."

Before Gwen could comprehend fully what she was being told, the other policeman added, "We need you to sign a statement that we've notified you as next of kin, and that you've received your husband's belongings. The car will be returned once we have finished our investigations."

Gwen felt thoroughly confused and sick to her stomach. It was an appalling message, and yet maybe she had caused him to do this because of her treatment of him. The death was therefore not only totally unexpected but caused a great deal of shame and grief.

Eventually she managed to ask, "Was there a suicide note or any explanation?"

"Nothing," answered the policeman, "although he did leave a book on the back seat with a piece of paper marking a page that described a suicide. We'll keep looking for the body and let you know if we find it."

There was nothing more that Gwen could think of to ask, as she was in shock. She explained to the policemen the state of her husband's health, his financial difficulties, and how he had acted out of character by leaving home so early that morning. They took notes, thanked Gwen for the information and had her sign a receipt for the suitcase.

When Gwen called George's parents to share the awful news, they were equally shocked and added to her feelings of guilt by politely suggesting that her treatment of him might have contributed to the cause, so she was infuriated by their reaction. She gave her son and daughter the news that evening, and they spent their time consoling their mother while everyone worried about what would happen next.

The following day, Gwen and her son went to the office to start winding down her husband's business, only to discover that George had taken out enormous loans against the family home, so it would have to be sold quickly and they would need to find somewhere else to live.

Gwen also found in her husband's desk correspondence referring to the Yorkshire court case, but it contained very little that she did not already know. There was, however, a short letter from a woman and a picture of a small boy that had been sent many years previously by the organisation for which George had worked in Yorkshire.

Everyone expected to hear that George's body had been found, but nothing was discovered. To Gwen, it appeared that her husband had chosen to end his life for a multiple of reasons: his business was failing, the relationship with his wife was broken, and maybe he was haunted by the knowledge of the woman and son that he had left behind in Yorkshire.

CHAPTER 16

In Yorkshire, it was the autumn of 1956, and my goal was to put my son's education back on track. The last thing I wanted was for him to fail during his second year at grammar school and be reassigned to a secondary modern institution (one that educates pupils who have failed grammar school examinations). I called the school secretary and arranged an appointment to see the headmaster. I found him very charming, and I think he saw me as attractive.

He sympathised with me and suggested that I assist my son by joining the Parent-Teacher Association. I agreed, and in the summer of 1957, much to my amazement, the school association elected me as its Chairwoman. It was a frightening experience. I had to stand in front of parents and deliver lengthy speeches about things that I knew nothing about and which challenged my confidence and oral communication skills. The headmaster calmed me down before my maiden speech by telling me to speak with enthusiasm, and to keep looking at the clock at the back of the room. I did, the strategy worked, and soon I was persuading parents to organise and participate in fund-raising events. Henry did not like my participation, however, and he mocked my efforts by claiming that I must be having an affair with the headmaster. Notwithstanding his hostility, John made progress and stayed on at grammar school after his second year.

My relationship with Henry, which had never been much fun or very satisfactory for me, continued to deteriorate, even though I had given him two more children during the first half of the 1950s, and after we had left the farm. During spring 1957, the court sent me copies of correspondence they had exchanged with George Luckett in which he had advised the magistrates that he was unable to pay child support because of his illness. That made Henry even angrier, and he insisted that I end John's education at age 15 and send him out to work. I refused, and it is fair to say that from that point onwards he despised me and would not forgive me for the way I protected my son. The only person who seemed sympathetic to my predicament was the school headmaster, who processed the paperwork to grant John free school meals indefinitely.

Henry's management of his diabetes grew more erratic, and it was with greater frequency that I found him collapsed outside the home after he had undertaken physical work that was inconsistent with the amount of insulin he had taken. It was not unusual to discover him lying on the ground with the tin full of sugar lumps I had given him still in his pocket, unopened. I was careful with his diet, especially the amount of carbohydrate he ate, and there were times when I had to drive him to places because he feared falling into a coma if he drove by himself. I also had to look after his treatment paraphernalia, such as boiling the metal and glass syringe he used for his daily injections, helping with his urine tests and reordering bottles of insulin. Life was very difficult, but I tried to avoid him having to be hospitalised.

I heard regularly from both of my married sisters, but it was the older one who brought me the most interesting news. She kept me up-to-date on the status of the airfield and how it had been re-occupied by the Royal Air Force after the US military, posted there for the Korean War, had moved on. The latest plan was to use it to house Thor missiles, and once again the local people were objecting. There was also news from her husband's neighbours that their daughter was still living in America, that her child was now of school age and the family was hoping to visit them very soon. My older sister was the only person in addition to my parents who knew about George Luckett, and she reported that he had not been seen since shortly after the war ended.

I told her that I had sent him a photograph of John via his employer's wartime address but had received no reply.

* * *

My son John celebrated his fifteenth birthday during May 1959 as a member of the school fourth form, and I continued my refusal to take him out of school at the end of the academic year. The Sunday after his birthday I was in a field near my home picking up Babycham bottles, Britvic juice tins, beer cans and the occasional empty container of spirits. We had held a school fundraiser dance the night before, and around 200 people had turned up to enjoy the open barbecue. Another 1,000 tickets had been sold, and before the event was over we had raised enough money to fund the purchase of a school mini-bus to be used for field trips and holidays. This morning, the two deserted marquees stood a few feet away, their white canvas coated with early morning dew, waiting to be dismantled. One had been used for dancing and the other as a bar, and the open barbecue stood in the centre of the field under a lime tree. The farmer opposite had allowed us to use his field for parking, and I had found nearby a cattle-dealer who owned a garage and had sold us the mini-bus at cost price. I took great pleasure in the praise I received from the headmaster.

At one stage, my husband threatened to disrupt the event by releasing livestock into the barbecue field, because he was so angry about my decision to keep my son at school. I became boiling mad and told him, if he did that, I would walk out on him with my son and leave him to take care of the other children. He knew I meant it, so he backed down, but he was still very angry.

I was not sure what my son should do when he grew up. Early on, a friend had tried to teach him the violin, but we quickly realised that his future did not lie in being a member of an orchestra. He developed into a keen cricketer, however; he played for two local village teams and apparently was very good, so there was talk that he should turn professional. Therefore, I arranged for him to attend a week's net practice with the Yorkshire Cricket Club, but unfortunately they pronounced that his fingers were too short for him to develop into a first-class spin bowler. Therefore, my last resort was education. The headmaster told me that he had done all he could to help, and it was now up to my son to make the effort if he wanted to succeed.

That summer I discovered that, in addition to his free school meals, my son was also entitled to a summer holiday with other underprivileged children at a seaside resort free of charge. This year it was six nights at a youth hostel in Saltburn, on the north-east coast of Yorkshire, and I took John to board the bus. He knew no-one except for a colleague from his school who was of mixed race and whom he thought was very successful with dating the local girls. He was one of the 2,000 so-called British "brown babies", born to white British mothers and black American GIs who stayed behind in Britain.

When I arrived at the bus depot, I discovered that local press and radio reporters were present and interviewing some of the 20 or so teenagers and their parents, and they would publish their reports during the evening news and in the following day's newspapers. I did not want the publicity, so for 30 minutes John and I hid behind the bus until the driver started the engine and prepared to depart, and I was very relieved that the published reports did not mention my son.

Dot Daniels continued to look after me, and I was always very grateful for that support. She knew I was struggling for money and continued to supply me with used school clothes that my son could wear. Most garments were tagged with the name of Dot's neighbour's son, but his first name was John, so I could cut off the surname and no-one knew that they were not originally purchased for my son.

One day when I visited her, Dot told me she had also arranged free haircuts for John. She knew a local barber who competed in male hairstyling competitions and needed boys on whom to practice, so she had volunteered my son. For the next few years, John regularly received free haircuts on Thursday evenings, as long as the barber was allowed to choose the hairstyle. John would walk to the hairdresser's after school, then stay with Dot afterwards until I collected him. The barber apparently told John that there was a problem with the shape of his head—an elevated bump on the back of his skull—that made him unsuitable for competitions, but he was a suitable practice model.

My biggest worry was whether or not my son would make it into his school's sixth form. The headmaster told me that he had done all he could to help John, and it was now up to my son to show that he wanted to succeed. I came up with the idea of monitoring his study hours and rewarding him with cash for the effort he put into his homework. He agreed to keep a record, and I paid him a pound for every fifty hours of study.

Henry remained enraged that I would keep my son at school after the age of 16 and insisted that his education was a waste of time. His dislike of John was ever-present, and it was in even greater evidence during the winter months when he entered the room in which my son was studying and turned off the electric fire, insisting that my son was wasting money. John persisted with the programme, however, even when he had to wear an overcoat to stay warm in his own bedroom, and by the narrowest of margins he passed a sufficient number of 'O' Levels (Ordinary Level exams taken in Britain marking the end of the secondary education cycle) and was invited into the sixth form. I was very proud of his achievement.

As a reward, in the summer of 1960 my father bought John his first car, a 13-year-old Wolseley 'Eight', which was a black, four-door sedan with an opening windscreen. The car did not go very fast, and the handbrake was suspect, but it was a big improvement over a bicycle.

My son and I practised his driving skills ahead of his seventeenth birthday, the day he would qualify for a provisional driving licence, by using one of the many derelict World War II airfields that surrounded the village in which we lived. I was patient with him, he listened carefully, there was nothing to run over on the wide runways, and it was enjoyable being away from Henry. A few weeks after his seventeenth birthday, he passed his driving test at the first attempt. Regrettably, my father could not help him celebrate as he had passed away during February 1961, just weeks before John's seventeenth birthday. This caused my mother to look to me to be her primary caregiver, despite the harshness of the life into which she had led me and the many demands on my time.

By now, my son was in the sixth-form and I could no longer help him with his studies. I received reports that he was making good progress, and that he had chosen out-door subjects to study, such as biology, geology and geography, which I presumed reflected his rural upbringing. During some weekends, he would disappear in his car to visit various nature reserves, especially Spurn Point Bird Observatory on the south-east coast of Yorkshire, and he talked about mist-netting, ringing migrant birds and adding new bird species to the life list of the ones he had already seen.

For myself, I continued to develop my employment skills by participating in a range of seminars organised by the Women's Institute, and volunteering in local hospitals so that I would be able to use my nursing skills to qualify for work if that ever became necessary. It was a long time since I had managed canteens during the war, but one day I hoped I would restart my career and demonstrate my competence to others, especially to my mother.

At the end of my son's two years in the sixth form, he passed all his exams and was given a place at the university that ranked number one on his selection list, but there remained one obstacle: a financial one. While his education was free, and he would receive a maintenance grant from the government, he needed money to support his student living, so he and I agreed that he should delay a year before starting university. Using my hospital contacts, I found him a job as a hospital porter that I thought would develop his work discipline and assist with his social development, since he had been brought up in such rural surroundings.

A year later, at the end of August 1963, my son was ready for university life. I drove him to his lodgings in Hull, stopping on the way to visit a relative of my mother's who I hoped would keep an eye on John, but in the end he did not. I found it extremely difficult to say goodbye to my son, and to bear the enormous sense of loss I felt at concluding our close relationship, but I consoled myself with the thought that it was what I had endured such hardship and spent so many difficult years fighting to achieve.

On my way home, I reflected on the 20 years of adversity I had experienced, from that awful night in my mother's home to hearing the melody and lyrics of Schubert's *Ave Maria* as my child was being born, the fight to avoid him being adopted, followed by the ups and downs of tending to a sick husband. At all times during my life, I continued to stop and listen to *Ave Maria* whenever it was played.

I had found strength in my faith and my commitment to God, from attending church during my childhood with Henry's first wife, to caring for my landlady's husband every Sunday in Leeds, to being denied access to church during my pregnancy, to my intermittent attendance while on the farm due to the weather and unpredictable health of my spouse, to the regular attendance in the village church once we moved off the moor. Here I had become a church warden (a liaison between parishioners and the clergy) as well as the organiser of the Sunday School. I had no regrets for not having my son adopted, but I kept no prayers for his father who had refused to provide any form of support.

I ended up by concluding that, now my son was no longer at home, I must focus my attention on his brothers and sisters.

CHAPTER 17

It was 22nd March 1957 in San Francisco, and there had just been a 5.7-magnitude earthquake centred in nearby Daly City, the worst to affect San Francisco since 1906. Eight-year-old Emma hurried home to tell her mother that she had hidden under her school desk during the lunch break until the teacher had told her to come out, and the school had closed early. She found her mother at home, still scared by what had happened and worried about the refrigerator door that had flown open and the water heater that was shaken off its wall mounting.

Michael was at work, helping with the construction of the city's Central Freeway, and reassured his wife when he returned home that earthquakes like this were very rare. He spent a fair amount of time away from home because of the many statewide infrastructure projects in which he had become involved. State investment was focused on road improvements, expanding water supplies, power generation and more school facilities to take care of the rapidly increasing population in California. In particular, he was involved in drilling under the San Francisco Bay to Oakland the first tube that would serve the high-speed electric train system (BART) that was about to be installed. There was also the city's network of freeways, including Interstate 280, that was built before the early1960s public revolt against San Francisco freeways.

The family decided to stay where they were living for schooling reasons, and Alice settled into a routine of taking care of her daughter and being at home for her husband. They discussed having more children, but it never happened. Contact with Alice's family in England continued through correspondence and the occasional telephone call, and she heard that her parents were retiring from farming and moving to a bungalow in the adjacent town.

In spite of Michael's work, the family still took time off for recreation at local destinations. In the early days, this meant spending time on the Russian river, but as the hippies took over, the family preferred Ben Lomond, Santa Cruz and Carmel. There were also road trips to South Shore, Lake Tahoe where Michael gambled in the casinos and Alice and Emma swam and sunbathed. During the journeys to the mountains, he would sometimes collect his parents in Sacramento and have his mother and father stay with them for a few days.

The 1960s evolved into a decade of war and destruction as well as "flower power" and the hippie generation. There was the Cuban Missile crisis in 1962, the Cold War with Russia, increasing violence in Vietnam, the assassination of President Kennedy in November 1963, of Martin Luther King in April 1968 and Bobby Kennedy during June of the same year. Concurrently, the hippies brought with them a culture of love, sharing and caring that they believed would cure the problems of the world, and that offering a flower would make everything turn out all right.

Both Michael and Alice still loved music, and listened to the Beatles, the Beach Boys, The Temptations, The Doors and The Byrds, although dancing had taken a back seat for the couple because of family obligations. Emma began to develop her own friendships, and as she moved into high school, she began to participate in the city's social scene. Both parents were concerned for her welfare, since she was an only child, but her behavior stayed modest and she listened to her parents.

By the age of 16 in 1965, Emma had developed her own circle of friends and spent much of her time outside the home. She remained in High School but was planning to continue her education by entering the nearby San Francisco State College. Her mother took her to see Princess Margaret and Lord Snowdon, visiting San Francisco from the UK during early November 1965. It was a curious affair with flashing red lights, news media and photographers everywhere, the visitors holding onto a trolley car for dear life, and the special privilege of travelling across the Bay by hovercraft to Oakland airport.

Emma did not go into the city centre very often, preferring to stay closer to home, hanging out at Donovan's Reef where dancing was prohibited but music was not, spending time on the beach with school friends and visiting the Doggie Diner near the San Francisco Zoo to eat under the dog's head with its sardonic grin. She smoked an occasional cigarette and drank wine, but otherwise stayed away from the hippie scene in Golden Gate Park and the gay and lesbian community in the Castro.

Soon she sought more independence and looked for new experiences, spending less time with her parents and more with her friends. She experimented a little but tried not to cross the line from right to wrong. She joined the Westlake crowd and participated in their parties and dancing in the basements of their homes, going with friends to the downtown Fillmore Auditorium or Avalon Ballroom and using the names of people she knew to gain free entry, and experimenting with marijuana. While some of her friends became funny, relaxed and creative as a result, she was upset when she encountered emotions of fear and delusion.

She thought about trying LSD or "acid", a mood-changing chemical, but was discouraged when she saw what happened to several friends. One was a girl whose older brother had returned from the war in Vietnam, only to be killed in a road accident a few days later. Her friend's grief was such that she overdosed on LSD to the extent that she imagined she saw her brother standing out at sea, and she walked into the ocean to recover him. Fortunately, others were watching and interceded to stop her drowning. Another friend, who had managed to get into the Fillmore with Emma, took two tabs of acid and decided to throw herself off the mezzanine in the belief that she could fly. Fortunately, again, several people ended her hallucination by grabbing hold of her and ushering her downstairs, from where Emma took her home.

Emma was greatly affected by these incidents involving her friends, and her resulting timidity induced her to stay away from the Summer of Love in San Francisco during June 1967. She had no wish to integrate with another reported 100,000 young people who turned up in San Francisco for the event, many of whom subsequently joined local communes. Instead, she and a friend went sightseeing in New York.

That same year, Emma enrolled as an undergraduate at San Francisco State College to study English and then become a teacher. It was a time of protest in higher education, and Emma quickly became affected by the longest and largest strike involving a California university. Even as she enrolled, there was growing dissatisfaction over racism and authoritarianism among the university leadership. At first there were just complaints and protest marches, but as the administration tried to suppress opposition through faculty suspensions and police intervention, the Third World Liberation Front took charge of the protests and a five-month strike took place between November 1967 and March 1968. There were rumours that the campus would be closed, which precipitated a desire on both sides to reach a settlement. Some classes continued, but few students attended because they had to pass through crowds of several thousand striking colleagues. An agreement was eventually concluded that created the College of Ethnic Studies and gave priority to creating a more diverse faculty and improving student admission processes.

Two years later, Emma's mother Alice complained of a headache that would not go away. At first it was diagnosed as dental problems, and then there was a suggestion that she had arthritis in her jaw, but finally the doctors traced it to metastacised lung cancer that had invaded her skull. Treatment was limited, and after radiation of her head, there was little else that could be done. Despite predictions of an early death, Alice battled the disease for two years before losing the fight. It was a sad time for Michael and Emma who struggled to resume her education and obtain her teaching qualification.

Emma had already graduated, having taken an extra year to qualify, but she stayed at home to help her father take care of her mother. Michael was overwhelmed with grief but thankful for his daughter's support.

As a measure of appreciation, Michael offered to take Emma to Europe to see her Yorkshire grandparents and relatives living in Belgium. The plan was to arrive in Belgium first, and then travel on to England where they would visit the places where Michael had worked during the war, ending up with her grandparents and the prison camp in the East Riding of Yorkshire. It would be Emma's first trip outside America, and she was delighted at the thought, although she had a lot of questions about the weather and understanding the way people spoke. They would fly to Brussels during August 1974.

CHAPTER 18

George Luckett's ferry from Weymouth to St Helier, the capital of Jersey, docked at lunchtime on a weekday during mid-April 1963. The island was a British crown dependency situated in the English Channel about 100 miles (160km) south of the English coast and 14 miles (22km) from the French mainland, with a land area of approximately 45 square miles (118 sq. km), and dimensions of 10 miles (16km) across and 5 miles (8km) from north to south. At the time of his arrival, it was home to about 62,000 residents. George had caught the first passenger boat out of Weymouth and was glad that the strenuous 36-hour journey was over; he had arrived in Jersey to live in exile, and no one in his family knew his whereabouts. He was weary of conflict and happy to have left his disagreements behind.

His adventure had begun early the previous morning when he left his house near Birmingham with the intention of faking his suicide and disappearing without a trace. His business difficulties had worsened to the point where he was unable to pay his debts and risked bankruptcy and possible imprisonment. His family life was not much better; his wife was forever complaining about his behaviour, she had forcibly committed him to a mental institution, moved out of his bedroom because of alleged violence and kept the children away from him to avoid his temper tantrums. At the age of 50, it was time for him to start a new life.

Careful preparations had been made. First, he had changed his name so that he could not be traced, then he had used his drafting skills to prepare paperwork that provided him with a new identity. Once out of the house, he drove to the Clifton Suspension Bridge, near Bristol, where he intended to fake his suicide. It was a favourite location for people who wished to end their lives, so he assumed that just one more death would not create any special attention. He would leave in the car materials implying that he had taken his own life, then park the car and find someone to give him a lift back to the city centre, with the excuse that his car had broken down and he needed a mechanic. If that plan failed, the alternative was to catch the bus to the train station about 3 miles (5km) away, although he worried that someone might see and remember him on public transport. Fortunately, he was given a lift.

Earlier, he had checked the timetable for trains travelling the Heart of Wessex route between Bristol and Weymouth. Weymouth was known to him because of his visits with his children when they were growing up. He would stay overnight at a guest house, but not one that he had used before, and the following day he would take the first ferry to St Helier. Everything seemed to have worked out as planned.

He chose the island of Jersey for a range of reasons. He thought it was foreign territory and far enough away that no-one would think to look for him there, assuming they bothered to look anywhere. The island had its own rules and regulations that protected him from law suits filed by his creditors, and he enjoyed the scenery and relaxed way of life. It was sunny and warm, the people were friendly and there was very little crime. He needed money to live on, so without telling his wife, he withdrew everything he had in his bank account and cashed in his personal pension plan.

Now that he had arrived, he was not sure what to do. The number of hotels and guest houses had increased dramatically since his last visit, reflecting the island's success at attracting tourists, but it was early in the season, so there were plenty of rooms to let.

He quickly found a guest house offering bed and breakfast, only a short walk from the town centre and bus station, and he became their only guest. He told them he was a successful civil engineer who was looking for a change in life, that he was unmarried and, after a serious illness, had decided to start afresh in an outdoors environment like Jersey. His landlords were happy to talk to him about the island, but reluctant to answer some of his questions about the war when Jersey was occupied by the Germans. The landlady had been born on the island, but her husband came from Breton. They had met, fallen in love and married while he was in Jersey helping with the potato harvest.

They said the war had been a difficult period in their lives. They had watched as the British Armed Forces abandoned the island in late June 1940, taking with them English citizens, Jews and people who were citizens of Germany and Italy, as well as all army munitions, and left the islanders to fend for themselves. There was no public announcement of their departure, so the Germans were unsure whether or not the island was defended. They dropped bombs to see what would happen, and when there were no signs of resistance, at the start of July 1940 they told the population to place white flags on their houses and buildings, and paint prominent white crosses in public places. The islanders did so, and the island was occupied by German forces.

It was a terrible time; the islanders felt they were imprisoned on their own island, while the Germans insisted that all weapons had to be handed in, and they confiscated all cars and lorries, requiring locals to use bicycles or horses and carts to get around. It was illegal to possess a radio, as the Germans feared that the residents would listen to the British Broadcasting Corporation, and a curfew was imposed from 11pm to 5am. It was announced that any hostile act, sabotage or protest would cause the German Gestapo to take hostages.

The islanders watched with horror as the Germans prepared for Operation Sea Lion and the invasion of Britain, as men and large amounts of equipment arrived from Germany. Luftwaffe bombers would congregate overhead before leaving for England as part of the Battle of Britain. It was encouraging to see fewer aircraft return than had left, however, and the Germans apparently were concerned by their lack of progress. The invasion did not take place, and within a few months, fortifications were being built in the belief that the British would try to retake the island, but that did not happen. By late 1941 a series of underground passageways was being constructed to withstand air raids, and close to the end of 1943 the structure was converted into an emergency hospital with a fully-equipped operating theatre and 500 beds, to be used in the event of an invasion of mainland Europe. It was never used for its intended purpose.

The Germans were well-behaved and strictly disciplined, spending most of their time at their military facilities, and mixing with residents only when they went to the pictures or attended some sporting events. The worst time for the islanders came at the end of the war, when Allied forces by-passed the islands as they invaded Europe, so that Germany could no longer support its troops with supplies. As a result, both the Germans and the island's inhabitants were greatly exposed to hunger and cold during the winter of 1944/45. Soldiers allegedly resorted to shooting sea gulls, eating dogs and cats and horsemeat, and cooking the remnants of vegetables left out in the fields. Nonetheless, relationships between the Germans and islanders remained good, and in some instances love affairs flourished and babies arrived. After the war, many babies were placed in orphanages, along with other abandoned children, including those brought from the British mainland.

* * *

For his first few days, George borrowed a bicycle and visited the sights he could remember from his earlier visits, such as the clean, soft sandy beaches and bays around the island, Elizabeth Castle on its tiny island, Corbiere Lighthouse, the German fortifications that still stood as grey, solitary reminders of earlier times, and the rock fields and pier at La Rocque Harbour. Bicycling was new to George, and he was troubled by pain from the saddle and in his calf muscles. Consequently, he decided to replace his bicycle with a moped, a French-made motorised Mobylette.

During the evenings, he explored the pubs and occasionally attended cabaret clubs, although he tried to stay inconspicuous and unnoticed. He read the English newspapers and was relieved to notice that there were no reports of his disappearance.

One of the hobbies he had wanted to take up for a long time was painting landscapes. The sights of the island resurrected this desire, and he decided to pursue the hobby in the hope of selling his paintings to tourists as a means of increasing his income.

A problem occurred when he discovered that he could not stay on the island indefinitely without an approved residency permit. His landlady told him that, without a permit, he would be unable to buy or rent property, but this was an obstacle he planned to overcome by finding work that the resident islanders could not perform themselves. Tourism was an option, and he would probably be provided with tied accommodation, but it was too temporary and likely to be restricted to the summer months only. He contemplated a banking career, since the island had recently relaxed its financial regulations, but he did not have the experience necessary to be hired by a merchant bank. He also considered agricultural work, but that was also temporary, and usually attracted foreigners, not British workers, so he might become conspicuous.

Eventually, he found employment as a draughtsman, preparing technical drawings—an essential occupation at the time—to help firms involved in everything from building hospitals and schools to constructing reservoirs. In his spare time, he explored the island and began to paint, which he found he enjoyed because it had a calming and relaxing effect on him. He could express his thoughts and feelings in whatever colour he chose, and he needed no-one's agreement to paint in whatever style he liked.

At first, life on the island was perfect for George, but as the months passed by, his sense of loneliness and being unwanted increased, and the drafting work he was given became repetitive and boring; also, he was disappointed that his paintings did not sell as well as he had hoped. Lack of contact with his family increased his sense of isolation and sadness, and he was more irritable and impatient, but he ignored the signs of illness and believed that his feelings were normal, and he preferred not to spend money on medical care. Doctors' surgeries and non-urgent hospital services in Jersey were fee-based, unlike the free services under the National Health Service that he was used to back home, so he stayed away from physicians.

His relaxed life-style began to turn on him during early 1966, as living on a small island worsened his depression. He would be angry with himself when a painting did not turn out as he had hoped, or something happened to him that was unexpected. He began to feel claustrophobic, and his sense of freedom turned into an impression of confinement. He felt he needed to get away from the island, but he was anxious about the possible consequences if he left. Despite drinking more and suffering the headaches, blood pressure and random thoughts caused by stress, he did nothing to seek medical help. He began to wander around town and elsewhere, sometimes not knowing where he was going, and occasionally forgetting where he was, but he could become violent and enraged if approached.

One summer's evening during 1966, he was stopped by the island police while he was wandering around town, with no apparent destination that he could explain, and for no obvious reason. He appeared delirious and bewildered, and he was unable to remember anything except his name. The police took him to the emergency room at the local hospital (a service which was free of charge) and the doctors diagnosed amnesia. The only things George could recall in addition to his name was an address in the Black Country in central England and a telephone number.

The number turned out to be the home of George's parents at the house in which he had been brought up. His parents were utterly shocked to receive a telephone call from Jersey and could not believe what they were told, even though the description of the patient sounded like their son whom they had thought was dead. The hospital agreed to take care of the victim until his parents could send someone to collect him.

George's father asked a brother to fly to the island, and a few days later a rather pale and long-haired George arrived at his parents' home, with everyone still in shock at his sudden reappearance, but no-one was sure what do with George. His wife, Gwen, was contacted and given the news, but she could not comprehend what she was told either. She had no desire to meet him, and she was so disgusted by his deception and dishonesty that she refused to have anything further to do with him. She had been living with her son and her mother since her home had been lost after George was reported as having committed suicide, and her daughter had moved in with a maternal aunt. Gwen went so far as to tell her children, who by then were both married, that if they spoke with their father she would disown them.

Despite many questions, George could not remember anything about what had happened to him during the years he was missing. The doctor prescribed tranquilisers to settle his state of mind and to help recover his memory, and while his parents were ecstatic to have him home, they puzzled over what he had done and where he had been for the past three years when he was supposedly dead.

Thus he rested at home. He did not know that both his son and daughter had married, nor did he have any knowledge about his illegitimate son in Yorkshire who was about to graduate from university during July 1966. He had paid a heavy price for his transgressions and misconduct during the war.

CHAPTER 19

My son John had moved to Hull during September 1963, and I had his landlady's permission to call him weekly on the telephone. It sounded as though his studies were progressing well and he appreciated the company of his two fellow lodgers, one of whom came from London and the other from Bradford. The Bradford student seemed to choose to socialise rather than study, and dressed like a Beatle, with a black collarless suit, tight-fitting, pointed-toe shoes, and a "mop-top" haircut. He was bulky, short and difficult to understand, even for my son, because of his thick Bradford accent. John preferred to spend time with the undergraduate from London, as both were studying geography and he could understand what the Londoner was saying.

John no longer received free haircuts, and he purchased his own clothes now that he had a small income, and because Dot, who had done so much to help me with his upkeep during his early years, had died some time previously. I was proud of my achievement in steering him to university, and I thought George Luckett would be well-satisfied with his son earning a university degree. However, I had long ago decided not to disclose anything to my son about his birth, mainly because I thought it was in his best interests not to know, and also as I lacked the confidence to tell him.

Our telephone conversation on Sunday 24th November 1963 was particularly emotional because of President Kennedy's assassination the previous Friday. John's landlord had announced the news to his lodgers when they returned home on Friday evening, and they had all spent the weekend in shock.

John came home for Christmas, and once again he was employed as a hospital porter to earn money, while I adjusted my schedule to give priority to my two youngest children, and to attend to Henry who was becoming progressively more frail. Our two older offspring had by then left home, one to be a nurse and the other a farmer.

My husband's illness persisted into the New Year and the doctor visited on several occasions. Unfortunately, the diagnosis was uncertain and finally, on 29th February 1964, the doctor decided to have my husband hospitalised. Henry left home in the back of an ambulance, after saying farewell to his two youngest children aged 8 and 10, and I followed behind in the car to be sure that he was made comfortable and had all that he needed in hospital.

When I got back home, the telephone was ringing as I walked through the door. It was the hospital, and the news was awful. The physician had gone to examine Henry late in the afternoon and found him dead in bed. The post-mortem indicated that he could have died of several causes, and not solely because of his diabetes.

Although I had faced many challenges during the past 20 years, I had faithfully taken care of my husband. In some ways I had been trapped in the relationship, and while from time to time it was abusive, I considered that I had an obligation to stay with my spouse. Now, the sense of loss was overwhelming and I dreaded to think of the future. Maybe what I had was better than what was to come, and not knowing was the worst part. The church vicar consoled me and reassured me that I had been faithful to my husband and done everything I could to help him, and I quietly wept as I listened.

Arrangements were made for Henry to be buried next to his first wife. He had died at the age of 77, and now here I was, aged 41 and facing a new range of responsibilities. I still had two young children to support, and with limited financial resources left to me by my husband, finding employment was essential to maintain a basic standard of living. John still had two more years at university, and there was no way I would allow him to leave without a degree.

My mother's attitude towards me had become dramatically different from her treatment of me when I was pregnant with John, and she moved into my home to look after the children while I searched for a job. I was fortunate as my nursing studies, combined with the skills I had learned early in the war, and had since developed through my church and Women's Institute activities, resulted in the local hospital authority employing me as its Hospital Warden for the three largest hospitals in the group. This put me in charge of day-to-day staffing issues and operations, even though it was over 20 years since I had fulfilled similar duties.

I decided to try again to trace George Luckett, to let him know what had happened to me and to remind him that he still owed me child maintenance. The court told me that they had heard nothing from him since the late 1950s, and because I had only a partial address, I wrote to the Ministry of Pensions and National Insurance to see if they would provide me with his current details. However, I was advised that the information was confidential, and I had no way of knowing that at the time of my inquiry he was living in isolation on the island of Jersey.

The following year marked a unique occasion. My son reached the age of 21 in 1965 and I wanted to make his birthday a special event. While my mother looked after the children, I visited him and organised a party for about 30 of his friends at a local hotel on the outskirts of Hull. There was lots of dancing and singing, as well as eating and drinking, and I believe I made nonsense of the saying that "A Yorkshireman is a Scotsman whose generosity has been squeezed out of him".

Now that I was single, I felt that I had to do a lot of catching up on life, in addition to fulfilling my family responsibilities. The hospital work allowed me to take my daughter to school and collect her each day, and I transferred my young son to a boarding school. Gradually I was able to enjoy a new way of living that allowed me to realise my ambition to travel. The war and other events had interfered with this dream, but now the obstacles were removed. My children could be cared for by my mother, my younger sister agreed to deputise for me at work, I had the salary to indulge in my whims and, with careful budgeting, I could support an annual foreign holiday.

The first year was spent travelling with friends in Western Europe, and on this occasion I took my two young children with me. It was a wonderful introduction to a new life-style, which lifted my spirits and gave me hope for the future. The trip was followed by a cruise to Africa on my own, followed a year later with a trip to the Holy Land.

My only sadness was finding that the close relationship with my eldest son was weakening. In July 1966, I attended his graduation, but then he moved to live close to London and work for Ford of Britain. He had developed a serious relationship with a girl, and during August 1967 they married. Both he and his wife became committed to their careers and had little time to visit me in the north.

Then another important event in my life occurred. I had evolved close friendships with several doctors at work, and one of them invited me to attend a one-day conference in London. We stayed for an early dinner, and while dining, we were joined by two men, one of whom was called John. I soon discovered that he was very well off, had also lost his partner, and he and his friend had been attending the Earls Court Motor Show. He was a few years older than me, about my height, and physically trim except for a slight paunch, and he boasted a complete head of silver-grey hair. His most obvious characteristic was his extraordinary self-confidence, and he was very direct and even rude towards people. However, with me he was always caring and considerate, and we quickly developed an amiable relationship.

Soon we started travelling together; we took a cruise to Spain and Morocco, and the following year we sailed on the Queen Elizabeth II to New York, and then went onward by Greyhound bus across America. At the start of 1970 we spent time in the Channel Islands, and I had no idea at the time that Jersey had recently been the home of George Luckett. John proposed to me, we married during July 1970, and my eldest son gave me away. A magical new life had opened up for me, and at the insistence of my husband, I retired from work.

* * *

The relationship with my older sister had always been strong, and I owed her many favours for the times she had taken care of my eldest son John when he was a small boy. Whenever we talked, she usually asked me about Mr Luckett and wanted to know if I heard from him or knew what he was doing, and I repeatedly told her "no". She envied my travelling and asked if she and her husband could accompany us on one of our trips someday soon, as her son was old enough to take care of the farm while they were gone.

Such a trip was arranged, and on an autumn morning during 1973, the four of us prepared to leave on a 10-day holiday in Scotland. My sister and her husband arrived by car, bringing with them my mother, who would look after my home while we were gone. I was told of their arrival by my husband.

"Your sister's here and wants to know which bedroom your mother should use."

I came downstairs and told my mother to make use of my bedroom.

"Are you ready to leave the farm?" I asked my sister's husband, knowing that it was the first time he had been away for more than a day since he married. Clearly, he was excited about the holiday but a little apprehensive about leaving the farm in the care of his son.

"It had better be okay," he mumbled. "My son can milk the cows, and he'll have some harvesting to do, but at least the sheep are in the fields and can take care of themselves."

With that, we were on our way. We left the house at about 2pm and hoped to reach Berwick-upon-Tweed to spend our first night away. The following day, we would complete the journey to Aviemore in the highlands of Scotland, and my husband John was driving. Cars were his hobby; he always bought a new vehicle each year, and currently owned a gold-coloured Rover P6 saloon with the larger 3500 V6 engine. He was proud of it, but he thought it might be the last Rover he owned since the company had recently been acquired by British Leyland, which was a company that had a reputation for poor design quality.

We discussed various topics such as the Irish Republican Army that had detonated bombs in Manchester and London, and the Conservative government that was struggling to control prices and incomes. At one stage of the journey, my sister raised an unexpected topic.

"Do you remember Michael Fromm from the war years?" she asked me.

"No," I replied, as I could not remember him.

"Well, he worked at the airfield and married the daughter of the farmer who lived next door to my husband's parents. He's an American and took his wife back to live in San Francisco. His mother-in-law says he's coming to see her next year with his daughter. She hasn't seen her grandchild for a long time, and Michael's wife died a year or so ago. He wants to show his daughter the places where he worked during the war and is keen to meet old friends. His mother-in-law has asked if anyone knows the whereabouts of George Luckett, as Michael used to work for him. Your name came up because you worked in the canteen, and Michael would also like to meet you."

The invitation troubled me. I did not really know Michael Fromm, and any talk about George Luckett was potentially embarrassing if my relationship with him entered the conversation—in particular, because my husband knew nothing about the circumstances under which my eldest child was born. However, before I could say anything negative, it was he who spoke up.

"It sounds like a good idea. Tell her yes, and let us know the details of when they will be here."

"I think it's next September," my sister added, but I think she sensed my anxiety because she added, "Everything will be fine; you're doing a favour for a friend of my husband."

We made it safely to Berwick-upon-Tweed and stayed at a very nice guest house overlooking the North Sea. The following morning, we left early and crossed the border into Scotland, travelled north via Stirling and Perth, and eventually arrived at Aviemore. It was all new to my sister and brother-in-law.

Aviemore had been developed as a tourist resort during the 1960s following a fire that had burnt down the old Aviemore Hotel, and the new centre was opened in 1966. We did some hiking, watched highland dancing and inspected the new snow-ski facilities. Soon we were on our way back home and I heard that all was well on my sister's farm.

But not all was well across the country. We returned to an outbreak of war in the Middle East (the Yom Kippur War) that dramatically reduced the supply of petrol, and the British government was in dispute over wages with the miners, who were threatening industrial action. By 1st January 1974, the dispute was hurting the nation to the extent that the country had to be placed on a three-day working week that lasted into March 1974. It was a miserable time, with power blackouts, food shortages and many people losing their jobs. We remained at home until the dispute was over and a new government was elected. As soon as order was restored, we drove down to see my son John and daughter-in-law, as their first child had recently been born.

Unfortunately, my life was not to remain distress-free for much longer. During July, my husband and I took a day trip to Scarborough on a cool, sunny day that allowed us to be very active, climbing the hill to inspect the castle, taking a boat cruise and walking along the sea front to the North Bay beach. All the damage I had witnessed during the war had long since disappeared, and we thoroughly enjoyed ourselves.

The following morning, my husband complained of chest pains while lying in bed, and to my horror, within a few minutes lay dead in front of me. I panicked, as nothing remotely like this had ever happened to me before, and I was at a loss to know what to do, so I screamed for help from my youngest son. He took charge and called the doctor, who in turn called the funeral home. I have to say that kissing my husband goodbye as he was taken from the house that morning was the saddest experience of my life.

Condolences poured in, my family returned to look after me, including my son John, and the funeral was arranged in my husband's home town. Afterwards, I felt truly alone. All my children were now working, except for the youngest who was away in London training to be a children's nurse. My mother took care of me until I was invited to visit France with some friends.

First, though, I had to fulfill my promise to Michael Fromm that I would meet him and his daughter to reminisce about the war. I now vaguely recalled Michael from his days at the airfield and how he and George Luckett would often be seen together. My biggest concern remained that my relationship with Mr Luckett might be brought up.

It was possible that he had said something to Michael Fromm after the bedroom incident but then demanded absolute secrecy when my pregnancy was discovered. My sister assured me that was very unlikely and she would accompany me to the meeting; I still had my doubts about the wisdom of it, but I did not think I could retract my promise.

CHAPTER 20

THE PLAN WAS to meet Mr Fromm and his daughter at an hotel in the town where his mother-in-law lived, but she would not be present. It was about an hour's drive for me, and I collected my sister from the farm on the way. We arrived at the hotel about 7pm, and Michael and his daughter were already waiting for us in the dining-room.

As soon as I saw Michael, I did remember him from 30 years earlier. He was still trim, but he had suffered substantial hair loss, and what was left had turned grey. Wrinkles were widespread across his face, thanks to working outside in the California sun, although he was clean-shaven and wore glasses which made him appear both serious and intelligent. I remembered him as well-dressed, but tonight he was wearing casual clothes. His daughter had the good looks of her mother, especially the soft dark hair and porcelain complexion that had been protected by her living under the cool, foggy, summer San Francisco weather. She smiled as we entered the room, Michael shook our hands and then invited us to have a drink.

I ordered a gin and orange, and my sister chose a sweet sherry. Our host drank beer and his daughter sipped white wine, as Michael told us that they had driven up from London a few days earlier. The hotel dining room was small, quaint and quiet, and it served traditional English fare—roast meats, fried fish, pies and pasties. Our meals were ordered before the conversation began.

"Thank you for being here," Michael began. "It's been a long time since I was at this place, and you're the only people I've found that I knew back then. I've shown my daughter where I worked, but until tonight she's not met anyone from my past."

"We're pleased to be here," my sister assured him, "but I'm not sure how we can help you. The airfield is closed, and everyone we knew left a long time ago, so tell us why you decided to return."

Michael explained: "We came because my wife died about a year ago, and Emma's grandparents are getting old and wanted to see their granddaughter. Also, it's a nice way for me to celebrate my daughter's first year of teaching."

We congratulated Emma on her work and asked about her family life. Her reply was almost apologetic.

"It's been hard on my father this past year because I've been living with his parents while I taught third grade in Sacramento," Emma said. "He's been lonely without me, although he has visited Sacramento fairly regularly. We both miss my mother, and coming here gives us time to spend together and celebrate her life."

My sister changed the subject in order to avoid creating further sadness. "Tell us what you've seen so far," she asked.

Michael took charge. "I've been to my old stomping grounds," he said, "but I'm disappointed that they've all fallen into disrepair. Yesterday, at the airfield, I could hardly recognise anything; the buildings are derelict, there's grass growing out of the runway, and all around you see rusted equipment.

"It was the same the day before. We visited my old prisoner-of-war camp and it's also abandoned. The sleeping huts look like I remember them, but the site is a mess, and the same was true of the American air base we visited near London."

"But what about meeting people from the past?" my sister was curious. "Did you manage to get in contact with any of them?"

"Only my old boss at the address he gave me years ago, but I received no reply. You're the only ones I've managed to find so far," Michael replied, sounding rather glum.

His daughter decided to lighten up the conversation. "Nevertheless," she said, "we've had lots of fun together. He's spent hours walking me around old places like York, Cambridge and London, explaining the history and telling me what I was looking at."

"I don't really remember you from the war," I interjected, looking at Michael. "Do you remember me?"

"I didn't know you well enough to speak to you at the airfield," Michael said, "but when I was with my boss, George Luckett, we would see you around the canteen, and then suddenly you disappeared. George also vanished while I was working down near London, and I've heard nothing since. I wanted to track him down during this visit."

"*So do I!*" I thought to myself. "*He could pay the years of child support he still owes me*," but I made no comment, except to say that I did not know where he was, and I had known him only because he had lodged with my parents.

It was then that Michael surprised both of us by producing a newspaper clipping and reading it:

"*Man Found Dead in Car*

"*A middle-aged tourist from England was discovered today dead in his car in eastern Yugoslavia. There was no sign of foul play, but investigations are continuing. The vehicle in which the deceased was found is a Ford Anglia Estate wagon. It was parked at a camping site frequently used by tourists visiting that part of the country. The body is believed to belong to a Mr George Luckett, whose home is in the West Midlands. His passport, wallet and personal belongings were recovered from the vehicle and his next of kin has been informed.*

"This is something I found while in London," Michael spoke enthusiastically. "I'm not sure it's our George Luckett, but it sounds awfully like him. It's weird that he should be in Eastern Europe. I'm thinking that, on my way back to London, I'll call at the address he gave me and see if I can track him down."

Then Michael delivered his final surprise for the evening.

"Would you two like to come with me?" he asked. "My daughter wants to stay behind with her grandparents and I would appreciate company on the journey."

The invitation was totally unexpected, especially coming from someone who was still very much a stranger, so I replied for both of us.

"I'm not sure that's possible, but let me and my sister talk about it and I'll call you in the morning."

Later, on the way back to my sister's farm she confessed she wanted to go. She had always been curious about Mr Luckett and liked the idea of tracing his whereabouts. Thus, the following morning, I called Mr Fromm and told him that we would accompany him. He was delighted.

The next day, with the early-morning ground mist rolling across the fields, we began our journey in Michael's car, heading first south and then westward to the West Midlands. Before we left, Michael called ahead to reserve two rooms in an hotel close to the address George had given him, as he thought it would be difficult to complete the journey there and back in one day.

I had never visited the West Midlands before. I knew Coventry and the East Midlands, but this part of England had never been a destination of mine. It was called the Black Country because of all the smoke and dirt emanating from the iron and coal industries and other factories in what was a highly industrialised area. The town towards which we were heading was known as an area of council houses and high-rise residential towers, and it was famed for its lock makers and key manufacturers. There seemed to be canals everywhere, and all the buildings were grimy and sooty. It was nothing like the green countryside I knew in Yorkshire.

We had the choice of two addresses to find. There was the one Mr Luckett had given me, but it provided only the town and the street name, not the number of the house. The address Michael had was given to him during the war by George himself, and it included the name of the house as well as the street and town. This second address was located a few miles to the east of the one I had, and it would be the first one we would pass, so we decided to start our investigations there.

When we found the house, it was imposing, detached and painted all in white, with an impressive driveway and what appeared to be a spacious rear garden. Michael knocked on the front door and a woman answered. After a brief conversation, during which there was a lot of pointing and gesturing, Michael scribbled something on a piece of paper and returned to our vehicle.

"George doesn't live there anymore," he announced. "The lady told me that the current occupants bought the house about three years ago when George's mother died. Apparently, she and her son were living there when she died and his father had passed away earlier. The woman gave me the address of a flat a couple of miles away where she says he moved to when the house was sold. She hadn't heard that he had died."

It seemed strange to me that George would be living with his parents when, as far as I knew, he had a wife and two children to look after, so I wondered: where were they?

We quickly found the new address, which was a small flat in a 20-storey tower block constructed during the mid-1960s, but the door was locked and there were no signs of habitation. We spotted a woman and her two children walking along an outside corridor, and Michael asked her, "Do you know who lives here?"

"I don't know his name," the woman replied, "but there's a man who's been living there for about three years, but he's usually away on holiday. However, I think he recently died and his family has been moving out his personal belongings."

Her answer prompted us to visit the building's caretaker where we learned that, indeed, the resident was the person about whom we had read in the newspaper. The caretaker kindly gave us an address, which he said was that of the man's wife who, apparently, with the help of her adult children, had been moving stuff out of the flat for the past few days. The address we were given was in a town a few miles away, out in the countryside, so Michael suggested that we postpone our search until the following morning and check in at our hotel because it had been a long, busy day, and he thought we would all benefit from an early night.

The following morning, after a large English breakfast, we set out to find the new address. It took us about thirty minutes to locate a nearly new semi-detached house with the traditional three bedrooms upstairs and three rooms below. Entry was through a side-door along a short cobblestone pathway, passing by a well-manicured expanse of green lawn.

The three of us walked up to the front door, Michael rang the bell and we waited. After a few moments, a woman appeared behind the glass, peered out and cautiously opened the door.

She wore a powder-blue dress, was aged probably in her mid-50s, about my height, a little stocky but not overweight; she wore large round eyeglasses and her brown hair, tinged with grey, had been permed.

Michael introduced us and then said, "I hope you don't mind us showing up like this, but I'm trying to trace a person I worked with a long time ago during the war. His name is George Luckett, and we are wondering if you are his wife."

Looking suspicious, the woman answered, "Yes, I was married to a George Luckett, but why is that important to you?"

Michael continued on behalf of all of us: "I am here from America trying to rediscover friends from the past. I worked with George at a Yorkshire airfield, and these two ladies who have come with me are the daughters of his landlady."

The last comment seemed to draw her attention, but she still had her doubts. However, she was curious enough to introduce herself as Gwen and invite us in.

"Although I'm George's wife," she said, looking from one of us to the other, "we've been separated for more than ten years, but I never divorced him, and if you don't know already, he died recently of a pulmonary embolism."

We nodded and followed her into the house. The progress we were making excited Michael, intrigued my sister, and intimidated me.

CHAPTER 21

THE PICTURES OF weddings and photographs of toddlers were the first things that caught my eye when I entered the sitting-room. None appeared to be of Gwen's wedding, and she read my mind as she saw me looking at the display.

"Those are my four grandchildren," she told me, "and the wedding photos are of my son's and daughter's marriages. They live locally, so I see them often; I have three granddaughters and one grandson, and the eldest has just turned seven. What about you?"

I told her that I had five children, the eldest two were married and, so far, I had three grandchildren.

Michael then explained who he was, including how he had recently lost his wife to cancer and had brought his daughter to England to spend time with her grandparents. He added that we two sisters who were accompanying him were known to him during the war, and we had agreed to keep him company during his search for George Luckett.

My sister then talked about her son and two daughters, and how they helped on the farm, but so far she had no grandchildren, and I added that I had recently lost my husband to a heart attack.

Gwen offered us cups of tea and promptly disappeared into the kitchen, soon to return with cups and saucers, a pot of tea, sugar and a jug of milk, plus a plate of biscuits.

Michael then resumed the conversation by saying, "First, my apologies for walking in on you like this. I had hoped to get together with your husband, but I have been unable to track him down until now.

I read a newspaper in London that reported his death, and I had an old address that he gave me when we were last together, so I used it to start our search in the hope of finding you. He often mentioned you and his two children. Can you tell us a little bit about what happened to him?"

Gwen began her story: "We had a huge falling out after the war when he contracted tuberculosis. I discovered things that he had never told me about, and while we tried to stay together, his behavior towards me was frightening and dishonest, and our marriage finally broke up during the early 1960s when he ran away to the island of Jersey. Earlier, he had opened his own business, but while he was at the peak of his profession, he couldn't handle the financial aspects of running a company, and slowly it fell into serious debt. I don't think he could cope with what was happening, so he would come home angry and frustrated. He often berated me and the children, and then, one day, he suddenly disappeared, with all of us believing that he had committed suicide."

"But that obviously didn't happened," interrupted Michael. "What did happen?"

"We'll never know the details. The police came to my house and told me he had jumped off the Clifton Suspension Bridge, but after several days of dredging the river, they didn't find his body. He left a financial mess, we lost our home, and I had to move me and the children in with my relatives. At the same time, I found a letter and a photograph in his desk revealing a relationship that he had with another woman in Yorkshire."

I could feel myself blushing, remembering the photograph I had posted to him. Gwen seemingly knew of my existence, and the presence of my eldest son, but so far she had not put the pieces together. It alarmed me that she might soon realise who I was, and confront me with some difficult questions.

"But he returned?" persisted Michael. "And then what happened, if it doesn't upset you to talk about it."

"It hurt me at the time," admitted Gwen, "but after ten years, I'm over it. I was furious when he turned up out of nowhere, and I told my children not to have anything to do with him. Both of them had married while he was gone. My daughter also had to give up her occupational therapy studies because of his disappearance. He wrecked my family and deceived me for a second time."

"So then what happened?" Michael encouraged her to keep going.

"He was found wandering around Jersey with amnesia; he couldn't remember anything, so his parents brought him home. I think he recovered fairly quickly once he was back, but I refused to have anything to do with him, and he moved in to live with his parents. I don't believe he ever worked again.

"I heard that he still suffered from temper tantrums and could be violent. On one occasion he apparently set fire to the garage, and he often ranted and raved against his mother over the tiniest of issues. There was clearly something wrong with him, but we never found out exactly what. He was prescribed medicine to control his behaviour, but often he didn't take it."

The storytelling was clearly exhausting Gwen, but she kept going.

"After he returned, he expected his mother to support him and therefore didn't need to work. His father died around the time he came home from Jersey, and his mother had to cope with his erratic conduct. Apparently, at one stage he decided to become a born-again Christian and look to God for his salvation. He had an awful lot to repent, but he became a regular churchgoer and raised money for the local church. This didn't last very long, though; he had a huge argument with the vicar over what the money he was collecting was being used for, and thereafter he never stepped inside the church again."

I wondered if his penitence also included what he had done to me, but Gwen resumed her story.

"His mother bought him a Ford Anglia estate car so that he could go touring in Europe, and I don't think he ever stopped travelling. The car had a collapsible back seat so that he could convert it into a bed. My daughter heard that he often took his violin with him and played on the streets to earn money."

Michael then referred to the newspaper article he had found, and said how strange it was that her husband should have been found dead in a car in Yugoslavia.

Without hesitating, Gwen replied, "It was during one of his many trips to Europe, and he would travel anywhere. I don't know that we'll ever learn what really happened. Apparently he was passing through Yugoslavia on his way to Romania. I can't imagine why he would want to go there, unless it was because of the new Romanian President, and he thought the country would be friendlier than it has been in the past. Anyway, he reached the border and tried to cross it, but the guards wouldn't let him through, and a terrible argument took place. He lost his temper when they turned him back.

"He returned to the original campsite and told another tourist what had happened. The following morning, the same person found George dead inside his car, and the authorities were called. The diagnosis was death by natural causes, and his body was flown back to England. Since I'm the next of kin, and both of his parents are dead, it was my responsibility to make the funeral arrangements. He was cremated and his ashes taken to the church in the village where he built the house that we lost when he disappeared to Jersey. The village was his favourite place. I asked the vicar to scatter his remains on a windy day across the churchyard so that they would land in no particular place. Since then, I've been cleaning out his flat. He had all sorts of stuff stored away, including films from the early 1950s."

We could sense that Gwen was exhausted by all her story telling, so we thanked her and Michael expressed his sadness that her spousal relationship had been so difficult. He added that it was a very different George from the one he remembered so well from the war, as at that time he had been very professional and someone who cared for his family.

Now it was Gwen's turn to ask questions. I anticipated that this was going to be the difficult part of the conversation for me.

"So are you the two sisters I met at my husband's lodgings when I visited him in Yorkshire at the beginning of 1943?" Gwen wanted to know. "I remember your parents, but you were in and out of the house while I was there."

My sister replied, "Yes, I remember you, but the other person was my younger sister. Frances Mary was working in Leeds at the time."

"Then, do either of you know who the women was that my husband had an affair with while he was building the airfield?"

I could feel my face turning red with embarrassment. There was no alternative but to confess and discover if Michael knew more than he so far had admitted.

"I was that person, although it wasn't an affair," I timidly announced.

Gwen looked amazed and seemed to be lost for words.

Michael was the first to comment. "I'm shocked. I knew from time to time he could flirt with the girls, but I never knew it reached this stage."

"It wasn't an affair," I repeated. "He molested me one evening in his bedroom and, as a result, I became pregnant. It was an awful time, for me and for my parents, and while George at first helped me financially, he soon ran away and refused to pay any child maintenance. I managed to keep the baby by being pushed into another relationship by my parents, which meant sacrificing my career, but I've survived and I'm proud of what I have achieved for my son."

My sister corroborated my story, but I think both Michael and Gwen were dumbfounded, and Gwen remained in shock for several minutes. I wondered how she would react, and if she would consider me to be a scarlet woman or pity me. It turned out to be closer to the latter.

"I'm shocked and disgusted," she said when she had finally regained her composure. "I learned of the affair when my husband was in the sanatorium, and he blamed you. He never admitted that it was an assault, and I never knew that he had abandoned you financially, as well as personally. I'm so sorry."

I thanked Gwen and reassured her that it had never been an affair, and we had never dated. In fact, I had hardly known him at the time of the incident.

"It was a long time ago and it's time to move on," I said. "I kept my son, my faith helped me cope, and now I've met you I realise that I was fortunate to know him only for a short time. Having recently lost my second husband, I need to get on with my life."

"But why didn't you trace him and make him help you?" Gwen wanted to know.

I admitted that I had tried, but if the courts had not succeeded, I doubted that I would be successful. Also, I had been trapped on a remote farm with no recourse to any legal help. My mother always blamed me, and the shame of the pregnancy stopped me from doing any extensive research. I had tried to contact him through a partial address, but I never heard back.

"Well, some of your correspondence arrived," admitted Gwen. "It appears he just didn't reply. What address were you using?"

I gave Gwen the address, and she told me it was the home that she and George had occupied after they were married in 1938. They had stayed there until 1961 when the family moved to the big house that George had built for them.

"Does your son know?" queried Gwen.

By now I was becoming weary of the topic and the amount of embarrassment it had caused me, so I told her no, I had no intention of telling him anything about his father or our meeting. "He's busy with his own life, and I don't need to upset him. It's a matter of leaving things as they are."

"I'm really very sorry for what happened to you," Gwen responded with compassion. "We both seem to have had our lives wrecked by George Luckett. When he first came home after the war, everything was fine, but that quickly changed, maybe because he was haunted by the secret he had left behind in Yorkshire. My children are also unaware of you, and I will keep it that way."

I thought it was high time to end our conversation, thank Gwen and leave. However, before we could depart she invited us to stay for lunch. I was relieved when Michael declined, suggesting instead that we should try to see the church where George's remains were scattered, and then start the long journey home. However, he told Gwen that, if she ever travelled to the United States, he would love to see her in San Francisco. Gwen told us that there was a very nice pub near the church, and if we had time, we should eat there.

It felt almost like make-believe to wander around the church, knowing that the person who had assaulted me many years earlier had found this location to be his final resting place. The red sandstone church had stood there since the eleventh century, and on the day of our visit the weather was sunny and warm as if to welcome us, so we did as Gwen had suggested and ate a pub lunch.

What an exhausting day! Michael had obtained the information he wanted, and a lot more besides, and I had discovered the history of the person who had abandoned me. I gradually came to realise that the day's findings removed many doubts and suspicions from my mind. George Luckett was deceased, and in the end he had not treated his family any better than he had treated me. Life with Henry had not been pleasant, and I had often felt angry at my mother for putting me in that position, but at least I had been able to keep my son, and I still believed that my husband's diabetes was the primary cause of his behaviour. His hostility towards John had not been personal but due to Mr Luckett's refusal to pay child support, and maybe because I kept John at school beyond the age of 15. I respected Gwen for what she had gone through, but I doubted that a close friendship would develop between us, due to our different backgrounds and because of living so far apart from each other.

* * *

As we drove back to Yorkshire, I speculated on what life might have been like had I not returned to my parents' home that day in August 1943. Michael and my sister reassured me that I had always done the right thing, and now I had the freedom to put my own personal life ahead of everything else. Michael said he had enjoyed my company and was sorry that it was time to say goodbye. He hoped I would visit him and his daughter in San Francisco sometime soon, and it would be his pleasure to be my tour guide

I also began to realise that I at last had alternatives and could make my own choices. I no longer had children to nurture, and my nursing qualifications and contacts were generating a surprising range of job opportunities, from child care for relatives of the royal family to live-in eldercare for a corporate executive. Where my reputation came from I was not sure, but it restored my confidence and self-respect. I was encouraged by a friend to record my first 50 years under the heading of "Frances in Flower", and once I moved to live in London, I revived my hobby of dancing. I was also living close to my son, John, and his family, and I began to see much more of them. All my children were independent, and my mother was always available to help me and give me a home in Yorkshire whenever it was needed.

I appreciated Michael's invitation and promised to visit him as soon as I could, as I hoped our friendship would develop. So far, my existence in this world has been challenging and turbulent, but now I look forward to a calmer, more comfortable and peaceful future.

EPILOGUE

As the author of this novel, I hope I have aroused your opinions on important issues described in this account. Had abortion been available at the time of my conception, would I be here to write the story? What consideration prompted my mother to refuse to have me adopted? Was it the message conveyed by *Ave Maria* or some deeper religious belief? Also, although she raised me, did her decision justify the disruption she caused to her own life and that of my father and his family? How do you strike a balance between the right to life and the right to choose? Was it justified for her to withhold the story of my birth from me for so many years?

There were uncontrollable chronic illnesses back then that affected the welfare of whole families, as well the events of the war which had a huge emotional impact, not least to do with the uncertainties of survival. In George's case, I wonder if his behavior was caused more by his genetic makeup or by the social influence of the times in which he lived. What might have happened differently had child support been paid? Should George have told his wife about the pregnancy at the time it occurred? What might have changed if he had done that?

Much of what you have read about Frances Mary and George is true. Names, places and some dates have been altered to afford a little privacy, but most of the main events did occur as described. Only Michael Fromm and the Air Commodore are wholly fictitious, introduced to bind the story together.

The two items of correspondence received from relatives and the one from Frances Mary's boyfriend at the time of her son's birth, and quoted in the novel, were actually written, and Dot Daniels was a real person. The baby expenses listed in the book are taken from my mother's notes, and Dot did supply her neighbour's son's clothing and arrange for free haircuts.

It was not until I was in my early 60s that my mother Frances Mary decided to talk to me about my origins. I was staying with her in London, and I did not know it at the time, but it would be the last time I saw her alive, as she died a year later. Most of the information she gave me turned out to be correct, although certain details were inaccurate. For example, Gwen was not a famous opera singer; she was the lead singer in the town's Gilbert and Sullivan opera society. Also, my mother used an incorrect name for George's son.

At no time during the evening of disclosure did I ask my mother why she had fought so hard to keep me, rather than have me adopted. I worried that this would upset her, and she might think me insensitive to the struggles she had endured to raise me. She was still ashamed of having been assaulted, and she swore me to secrecy and begged me not to research my past while she was still alive, and to keep confidential the information she had given me. An email she sent me a few days later stated: *"No John, I think you should not say anything at this point. One talks to another and in no time it is in Yorkshire."*

My mother's death was an opportunity for me to conduct further investigations. My father's real name was distinctive, so I was optimistic that I would discover more information. I tracked down his birth date and then obtained a copy of his marriage certificate. With the help of Ancestry.com, I also obtained a copy of my father's birth certificate, but then I encountered road blocks. As a result, I hired the help of a genealogist living in Ramsgate, England.

A few weeks later the genealogist began to have success. She reported that the details of my grandparents on my father's side had been found, and from there she had been able to confirm the birth of my father and also the birth of his older sister. She could trace his sister's marriage, the children who were born to her, and his sister's death, but it was difficult to track my father. All efforts to find a death certificate had been unsuccessful. She concluded that my father *"either did not die in Britain, or had died after 2005"*. From my father's marriage certificate, she was able to trace his two children, and could confirm their marriages and the names of their children, but she could not identify their whereabouts. Ultimately she traced a death certificate from 1993 that appeared to be my father's wife. It was assumed that the couple had not divorced because the person who died was listed as a widow; thus it was assumed that George was already deceased by that time.

We also checked with the UK Institute of Civil Engineers. They had no record of my father having been a member after the war, nor had any record of his qualifications. However, with further research they reported that he had been accepted as a student member in 1931, but his membership was cancelled during January 1942 because he was overage for student membership and had not changed his status with the Institute.

The Petty Sessions Court was also contacted, since it had exchanged correspondence with by father during April 1957. It checked its records from January 1956 to June 1958 but could find no reference to the case during that time.

With this information, it was now up to the genealogist to contact my half-sister to see if she would communicate with me. Miraculously, she agreed, and much of what is in the novel concerning George Luckett comes from her recollections. We have met on several occasions and continue to this day to be in close contact. She admits that at one point in her life her mother told her "you might have a brother in Yorkshire".

Several lengthy emails were exchanged between me and my half-sister, and I was shocked and amazed to learn about the difficulties my father had created for his family. The stories were unreal, the sort of stuff that people normally invent. It seemed as if my arrival in the world had spun him out of control, as well as dramatically affecting the life of my mother. The one overriding thought that kept returning to me, time after time, was the sense of appreciation for having been allowed to live.

A little while ago, I visited my half-sister for the first time and she helped me uncover a whole new side to my life. Before we met, she had worried about what type of person I might be, so her husband and eldest daughter had offered to be at the meeting with her, just in case, but she declined their offers. I was equally apprehensive about what I might find when I knocked on her door. In reality, I discovered a wonderful and kind person, someone you would be proud to call your sister.

On my mother's side, I am the eldest child, and on my father's side I am the youngest, and I confess that this sometimes gives me a strange feeling. Would my life have been different if I had known about my background sooner? I do not think so. I have always been independent and obstinate, and I believe I have inherited the intelligence of my father and the compassion of my mother. I am proud of my new family and continuously feel amazed that I am still here on this planet.

ANNOUNCING A NEW BOOK:
SHE WORE A YELLOW DRESS

BY NOW YOU will understand how this author arrived in this world and how his mother's dedication and courage allowed him to thrive and achieve a university education. What happened thereafter? What did he do with his life? How did this upbringing influence him? Did he ever discover the existence of his father? Was he able to develop meaningful relationships with other people? Did he suffer from the same health conditions as his father and how did he adjust to family domesticity?

The answer to these questions are to be found in the novel *She Wore a Yellow Dress*, and as with this narrative, it is historical fiction inspired by real-life events. It is a coming-of-age romance story that focuses on happenings in Britain during the period 1965 to 1975. It was a time of major economic and social transformation in Britain, when there was runaway price inflation, the country joined the European Common Market, militant trade unions opposed pay controls and limits on free collective bargaining, and the government was forced to impose a national three-day working week at the start of 1974.

Concurrently, the book tracks John's romantic relationships, his jealousies and stupidities, his struggles to decide on a career, the role that his spouse played in his advancement, the affection, tolerance and compromises that typified their marriage and the importance to John of birdwatching. Details of the novel's availability will be published on my website at: johnrcammidge.com.

www.ingramcontent.com/pod-product-compliance
Lightning Source LLC
LaVergne TN
LVHW012021060526
838201LV00061B/4403